Echoes of Mae

By

Seth M. Murphy

This book is a work of fiction, but is based on real life events. Names and details have been changed, but real life events inspired this story.

Chapter 1

The air in their small apartment had begun to hum with a new kind of energy, a quiet resonance that settled into the very walls. It was a feeling Shawn and Kate had only ever glimpsed in the periphery of their lives before, a soft melody played from a distance, but now, it was here, alive and breathing within their shared space. The news of the pregnancy had arrived not with a thunderclap, but with a gentle unfolding, like the petals of a flower unfurling to the morning sun. It was a shared secret, a whispered promise that, at first, they held close to their chests, a fragile hope cradled in the palm of their hands.

Kate's eyes, usually so bright and observant, now held a dreamy luminescence. She would often find herself staring, a soft smile playing on her lips, at the swell of her belly, a burgeoning universe within her. Shawn, usually grounded and practical, found himself caught in the same gentle current. His gaze would linger on Kate, a profound tenderness softening the edges of his features, an unspoken awe for the miracle she carried. He'd trace the curve of her abdomen with a reverent touch, feeling the faint, almost imperceptible thrum of life beneath his fingertips, a nascent rhythm that mirrored the beating of his own heart. The apartment, once a sanctuary of comfortable routines and shared laughter, began to transform. It was as if the very air was being re-sculpted, infused with the scent of possibility.

The soft yellow they chose for the nursery wasn't a decision made from a magazine or a Pinterest board; it was an instinct, a shared feeling that this color embodied warmth, sunshine, and the gentle embrace of new life. It was a shade that promised comfort, a blank canvas awaiting the vibrant hues of a child's world. Shawn found himself spending hours in the small room, ostensibly assembling the crib, but more often than not, he'd stand by the window, gazing out, his mind adrift in a sea of imagined futures. He'd picture tiny hands reaching out, hear the phantom echo of a baby's gurgle, and feel a protective surge that was both exhilarating and a little terrifying. Kate would join him, leaning against the doorframe, a knowing smile on her face, her own dreams weaving themselves into the tapestry of his. They spoke in hushed tones, their words laced with a delicate reverence for the unseen presence growing between them.

The name "Mae" had arrived with a similar, almost mystical synchronicity. It wasn't a name they'd debated or meticulously researched. It simply *was*. It felt like a song, a gentle, melodic phrase that settled into their hearts with an undeniable rightness. Kate would whisper it to her belly, the sound, a soft caress in the quiet of the room. Shawn would repeat it, testing its weight, its sound, and finding it perfect. Mae. It held a certain old-world charm, a delicate beauty, and a quiet strength that they instinctively felt would be her. It was a name chosen not for its trendiness, but for its soul, a name that felt as pure and luminous as their burgeoning hopes.

Their world, usually so grounded in the everyday rhythms of work, bills, and shared dinners, began to orbit around this nascent life. Stolen glances across crowded rooms became charged with a new understanding. A shared grocery run morphed into a whispered discussion about lullabies. The comfortable silence they once enjoyed now held a different quality, a vibrant expectancy. Even the mundane had taken on a glow, a soft luminescence that hinted at the extraordinary. Their small apartment, usually a testament to their shared history and comfortable domesticity, was becoming a hallowed space, a sanctuary where a new chapter of their love story was being written. The worn armchair in the living room, where Shawn often read, now felt like a perch from which to observe Kate, his silent guardian of the growing miracle. The kitchen, where they'd cooked countless meals together, now echoed with the soft hum of Kate's content humming as she prepared healthy snacks, a gesture of nurturing not just herself, but the life within.

The first flutter inside Kate's belly was a moment that transcended description. It wasn't a dramatic event, no fireworks, no grand pronouncements. It was a subtle shift, a delicate dance of existence that vibrated through Kate and, by extension, through Shawn. He had his hand resting on her stomach, his breath held captive, when he felt it. A tiny, insistent pulse, a whisper of movement that confirmed the impossible, the tangible reality of their child. Tears welled in his eyes, not of sadness, but of an overwhelming, humbling joy. Kate's hand found his, her fingers intertwining, a silent acknowledgement of the profound connection that now bound them, not just to each other, but to this new, tiny being.

These were the days of whispered dreams. Dreams of bedtime stories read in soft voices, of tiny fingers curled around their own, of the uninhibited sound of laughter filling their once-quiet apartment. They imagined a future painted in broad strokes of joy and endless possibilities. Shawn pictured himself teaching Mae to ride a bike, his hand steady on the seat, his heart swelling with pride. Kate saw herself braiding her daughter's hair, sharing secrets and giggles. These were not just fantasies; they were blueprints for a life they were building, brick by emotional brick, with an unwavering certainty that this was their destiny. The anticipation was a tangible thing, a sweet ache in their chests, a constant thrum of excitement that made the ordinary feel extraordinary.

They started small, these tangible expressions of their burgeoning family. Kate began sketching designs for a mobile, intricate patterns of stars and moons that would hang above Mae's crib. Shawn, with a newfoundpatience, took on the task of building a bookshelf, envisioning it filled with a lifetime of stories. Each brushstroke of yellow paint on the nursery walls, each carefully chosen baby blanket, each whispered name – Mae – was an act of profound love, a testament to a future they were meticulously crafting. The small apartment, with its familiar creaks and sighs, became a haven of burgeoning hope, a cocoon preparing to shelter the most precious of lives. The usual arguments about whose turn it was to do the dishes or which movie to watch seemed to fade into insignificance, replaced by a shared focus, a collective gaze fixed on the horizon of their future.

The world outside their intimate bubble continued its relentless pace, oblivious to the miracle unfolding within their walls. The demands of work, the occasional social obligations, the mundane worries of daily life – they all receded, their significance diminished by the overwhelming presence of Mae. This was their universe, a self-contained world of anticipation and love, a sanctuary built on the fragile yet powerful foundation of expectation. Shawn found himself walking with a lighter step, a quiet contentment radiating from him. Kate's radiance was undeniable, a physical manifestation of the joy bubbling within her. They were a portrait of serene expectation, two souls intimately connected, their love story poised to expand into something even more beautiful, more profound, with the arrival of their daughter.

This period, rich with the promise of new life, was deliberately etched in his memory, not just as a fond recollection, but as a stark and vital contrast to what was to come. It was a time of unadulterated joy, a period where the word "loss" felt as foreign and irrelevant as a word from an ancient, forgotten tongue. The tenderness with which they approached every aspect of the pregnancy, from the selection of paint colors to the whispered hopes for their child's future, was an embodiment of a love that was pure, unblemished, and utterly convinced of its own enduring strength. The tiny apartment, bursting at the seams with their dreams, was a testament to a love that was ready to overflow, a love that was preparing to welcome its greatest expression. Each stolen glance, each whispered lullaby, each gentle caress of Kate's burgeoning belly was a brushstroke on the canvas of their unfolding dream, a dream that was as vibrant and full of promise as the soft yellow they had chosen for their daughter’s sanctuary.

It was a love story beginning its most beautiful chapter, a chapter written in the language of anticipation, hope, and the quiet, profound joy of waiting. The sheer magnitude of that happiness, the unshakeable belief in the goodness of what was to come, would later serve as a critical counterpoint, a brutal reminder of the precipice upon which they stood, unaware of the sheer weight of what was about to be lost. The brightness of that time was not just a memory; it was a harbinger, a luminous beacon illuminating the depth of the darkness that lay ahead. It was a prelude, a symphony of gentle notes played before the first, shattering chord of tragedy.

Chapter 2

The day it all shifted, the day the dream began to fray at the edges, arrived not with a dramatic pronouncement, but with a series of urgent, clipped phone calls. The doctor's tone, no longer one of gentle reassurance, was now laced with a professional gravity that sent a jolt of fear through Shawn. Kate was admitted to the hospital, not for the joyful culmination of her pregnancy, but for observation. The cheerful yellow of the nursery, the carefully chosen name, the countless imagined moments – they all seemed to recede, replaced by the stark, sterile reality of hospital corridors and the hushed urgency of medical staff. The scent of antiseptic replaced the imagined aroma of baby powder.

Shawn's hand, which had so recently traced the gentle curve of Kate's belly with such tenderness, now gripped the sterile bedsheets, his knuckles white. He watched as the nurses moved with practiced efficiency, their faces a mask of professional detachment that offered little comfort. Every beep of the monitor, every rustle of a gown, every hushed conversation between doctors felt like a hammer blow, chipping away at the last vestiges of their carefree optimism. Kate's face, usually so open and expressive, was now etched with a weariness that went beyond physical exhaustion. Fear, a cold, unwelcome guest, had taken up residence in her eyes. She would reach for Shawn, her grip surprisingly strong, her gaze pleading for a reassurance he found increasingly difficult to offer.

The hours stretched into an agonizing eternity. The world outside the hospital room ceased to exist. Their meticulously planned future, once so vibrant and clear, had dissolved into a hazy uncertainty. Shawn found himself pacing the small room, his mind a frantic carousel of worst-case scenarios. He'd recall snippets of conversations, medical terms he'd barely registered before, now echoing in his head with a terrifying clarity. The gentle unfolding of their dream had become a desperate struggle, a fight against an unseen enemy that threatened to snatch away their most cherished hope. He'd try to speak words of comfort, but they felt hollow, inadequate against the weight of the unspoken fears that hung heavy in the air.

The delivery itself was a blur of white coats, hushed voices, and the piercing sound of Kate's pain. The joy that should have accompanied the birth of their daughter was overshadowed by a palpable sense of dread. When Mae was finally born, she was not placed in Kate's arms, not immediately. Instead, she was whisked away, a tiny, fragile bundle swaddled in sterile cloth, her cries faint, almost lost in the cacophony of medical urgency. A profound silence fell over the room, broken only by the frantic beeping of machines and the strained whispers of the medical team. Shawn's heart plunged. He looked at Kate, her face pale and streaked with tears, her eyes wide with a terror he mirrored.

The sterile, fluorescent-lit world of the Neonatal Intensive Care Unit, or NICU, became their new reality. It was a stark contrast to the soft yellow nursery, to the imagined warmth of their home. Here, life was measured in the relentless rhythm of machines, in the steady, insistent beep of monitors that tracked every precious breath. The air was cool, tinged with the antiseptic smell that now seemed to permeate everything. Rows of incubators, each cradling a tiny, vulnerable life, stretched before them, a silent testament to the fragility of existence. The hushed urgency of the nurses, their faces etched with a mixture of compassion and professional concern, created an atmosphere of constant, low-level anxiety.

Mae, their daughter, their Mae, was a tiny figure swaddled in blankets, her chest rising and falling with the aid of a ventilator. Tubes and wires, a delicate web of life support, connected her to the machines that were now her lifeline. Her skin was translucent, her features so delicate they seemed almost sculpted from porcelain. Shawn and Kate stood beside her, their hands hovering, afraid to touch, afraid to disturb the fragile balance of her existence. They had dreamt of holding their daughter, of feeling her tiny fingers curl around theirs, of gazing into her innocent eyes. Now, their connection was mediated by plastic and wires, their love expressed through silent observation and whispered prayers.

The medical jargon, once alien and distant, became a part of their everyday vocabulary. They learned to decipher the subtle nuances of oxygen saturation levels, the significance of heart rate fluctuations, and the implications of apnea alarms. Each term was a potential threat, a reminder of the precariousness of Mae's hold on life. The doctors, though kind and patient, delivered their updates with a clinical detachment that was both necessary and, at times, agonizing. They spoke of statistical probabilities, of potential complications, of the long road ahead. For Shawn and Kate, these were not abstract concepts; they were the raw, terrifying details of their daughter's struggle.

The bright hope of earlier days had not vanished entirely, but it had been reduced to a fragile ember, carefully guarded against the winds of despair. The soft yellow of the nursery, once a symbol of warmth and comfort, now felt like a distant memory, a relic from a time when their world was bathed in the simple, uncomplicated glow of expectation. The name Mae, once sung with such tenderness, was now whispered with a prayerful reverence, a plea for strength, for resilience. They would sit for hours by Mae's bedside, their hands clasped tightly, drawing strength from each other, from the sheer, unyielding force of their love for their child.

The NICU staff, in their tireless dedication, became both allies and a constant reminder of the gravity of their situation. Nurses with kind eyes and gentle hands would explain the procedures, adjust the tiny IV lines, and offer words of encouragement that, while appreciated, could never fully erase the gnawing fear. Shawn found himself developing an almost obsessive vigilance, his eyes constantly scanning the readouts on the monitors, his ears attuned to the slightest change in the rhythm of the machines. He would replay every conversation with the doctors, searching for any missed nuance, any hidden sign of hope or despair.

Kate, though physically weaker, possessed a remarkable inner strength. She would speak to Mae in soft, hushed tones, her voice a gentle balm against the sterile environment. She'd describe the nursery, the yellow walls, the mobile with its stars and moons, weaving a tapestry of the life that awaited her daughter. Shawn would join in, his voice rough with emotion, adding details of the stories they would read, the songs they would sing. It was an act of faith, a defiant assertion of their love in the face of overwhelming uncertainty. They were building a future, not with brushstrokes of paint, but with whispered words, with unwavering hope.

There were moments of intense despair, of crushing hopelessness. The sight of another tiny crib, empty, or the hushed tones of a conversation between doctors about another family's loss, could send them spiraling. The world outside the NICU seemed impossibly distant, its concerns trivial in comparison to the battle being waged within these walls. They lived in a perpetual state of suspended animation, their lives irrevocably altered, their focus narrowed to the fragile pulse of the tiny life before them. Sleep offered little respite, often invaded by nightmares that mirrored their deepest fears. Waking up to the relentless beeping of the machines was a constant, stark reminder of the reality they faced.

Chapter 3

The days got longer and longer. Each tiny gain – a slight increase in weight, a decrease in the need for oxygen, a moment when Mae stirred in her sleep – was celebrated with a quiet, profound joy that bordered on euphoria. These small victories were the fuel that kept their fragile hope alive. Conversely, any setback, any warning sign, sent them back into the depths of anxiety, their spirits battered and bruised. They learned to exist in this precarious balance, their emotions oscillating between the elation of progress and the crushing weight of potential regression.

Shawn, ever the protector, found himself channeling his fear into action. He learned to hold Mae, his movements slow and deliberate, his heart thrumming with a mixture of terror and overwhelming love. He would gently stroke her tiny hand, marveling at its impossibly small size, at the faint warmth that emanated from her skin. He would talk to her, telling her about their world, about the love that surrounded her, about the future they were fighting for. He found a strength he never knew he possessed, a primal urge to shield his daughter from the harsh realities of her early days.

Kate, in her own way, was equally fierce. She would read to Mae, her voice sometimes cracking with emotion, her eyes never leaving her daughter's face. She'd sing the lullabies she had practiced in her mind for months, her voice a fragile melody in the sterile air. She was a silent warrior, her love a shield, her determination a testament to the unbreakable bond between mother and child. The soft yellow of the nursery, the name Mae, the whispered dreams – they were not forgotten. They were the anchor, the beacon that guided them through the storm.

The once simple act of eating became a complex dance of careful measurements and watchful eyes. The nurses would meticulously prepare Mae's feedings, ensuring every milliliter was accounted for, every vital sign monitored. Shawn and Kate would observe, their breaths held captive, their hearts pounding with each successful swallow, each steady beat of her heart. It was a constant vigilance, a heightened awareness of every tiny detail, for in these details lay the hope for their daughter's recovery. The world outside the NICU, with its everyday concerns, felt like a distant planet, its gravitational pull weakened by the all-consuming reality of their daughter's fight for life. Their dreams, once painted in broad strokes of joy and boundless possibility, were now meticulously detailed in the small, precious victories of each passing day. The bright hope of the unfolding dream had been tested, battered, and reduced to a tenacious, glowing ember, kept alive by the unwavering flame of their love.

The silence that descended was not a gentle one. It was a brutal, absolute cessation of sound, a vacuum that sucked the air from the room, from their lungs, from their very souls. The rhythmic beeping, the hum of machinery, the hushed murmurs of the medical staff – all of it, suddenly, impossibly, gone. Replaced by a vast, echoing stillness that pressed in on Shawn and Kate, heavy and suffocating. It was the silence of a dream abruptly shattered, of a world that had abruptly, irrevocably, ceased to exist.

In that suffocating quiet, a nurse, her face a mask of practiced compassion, gently detached the last of the wires, the tiny tubes that had been Mae's lifeline. Her movements were deliberate, almost reverent, as if she understood the profound sanctity of this moment, the devastating finality it held. Shawn watched, his vision blurred, his own breath held captive in his chest. He saw the nurse place Mae back into his arms.

And then, he held his daughter. Truly held her, for the first time. Not through a plastic barrier, not with the apprehension of disturbing delicate equipment, but with the unadulterated, agonizing reality of her small, warm weight against his chest. Her stillness was profound, a stillness that spoke of an ending, not a rest. Her skin, so recently radiating that fragile inner light, now felt… inert. The warmth was fading, leached away by an invisible tide. He traced the delicate curve of her ear, the impossibly soft skin of her cheek, the tiny, perfect shape of her lips. These were the features he had studied for weeks, the details he had memorized, the ones he had promised would one day smile and laugh. Now, they were a tableau of silent perfection, a frozen moment of what might have been.

Kate's hand found his, her fingers cool against his, a stark contrast to the phantom warmth he was still trying to feel from Mae. She leaned her head against his shoulder, her body trembling, a silent testament to the seismic upheaval within her. Her whispered words were lost in the enormity of the silence, a broken murmur of "Oh, Mae…" that seemed to unravel the very fabric of their existence. Shawn could feel the tremor running through her, a mirror of the one he felt deep within himself.

Kate stirred, her voice a fragile thread in the stillness. "She's so… peaceful," she whispered, the words catching in her throat. Peace. It was a word that seemed utterly alien to the maelstrom of emotions swirling within them. Peace felt like a betrayal, a surrender to the absence. Their daughter, who had fought so valiantly, deserved more than a quiet, peaceful end. She deserved a life, a cacophony of joyful noise, a universe brimming with the love they had so freely offered.

Shawn tightened his grip, his knuckles white. "She's… perfect, Kate," he managed, his voice raspy, raw. Perfect. Yes, she was perfect. Perfect in her fragility, perfect in her brief, incandescent presence, perfect in her stillness. But perfection had never been what they craved. They had craved the messy, imperfect, glorious reality of a living, breathing child. The scraped knees, the tantrums, the boisterous laughter that would fill their home. The imperfections that made life real, that proved existence.

The weight of Mae's small body in his arms was a tangible manifestation of their loss. It was the physical embodiment of everything they would never experience. The first steps, the bedtime stories, the innocent questions about the world. He felt a profound sense of disconnect, as if his own body were no longer fully his own, as if a vital part of him had been carefully removed, leaving behind an aching void. He looked at his hands, the hands that had so longed to hold her, to comfort her, and they felt clumsy, useless, imbued with a chilling emptiness.

Kate reached out, her fingers brushing against Mae's cheek. A single tear traced a path down her face, catching the faint light and glittering like a tiny, fallen star. It was a quiet, solitary tear, yet it felt like the beginning of a flood, a prelude to the immense outpouring of sorrow that was yet to come. Shawn watched it fall, a silent acknowledgement of the dam that was about to break.

He remembered the doctor's words, delivered with a professional gentleness that had felt like a blow. "I'm so sorry," he had said, his gaze steady but kind. "We did everything we could." Everything. The word hung in the air, heavy with the unspoken acknowledgment of limits, of failures. Shawn had nodded, unable to speak, his mind a jumble of medical terms and desperate pleas. But now, in the suffocating silence, the futility of those efforts pressed down on him. All the advanced technology, all the skilled hands, all the sleepless nights – they had not been enough. The intricate dance of life had faltered, and the music had stopped.

The unreality of it all was a persistent, disorienting hum beneath the surface of their grief. It felt like a dream, a terrible, vivid nightmare from which they would eventually wake. But the stillness of Mae's small body was a constant, grounding anchor to this harsh reality. The coolness of her skin, the absence of breath, the profound silence – these were not illusions. They were the irrefutable proof of their loss.

Kate finally looked up, her eyes meeting his. There was a shared understanding in that gaze, a silent acknowledgement of the profound chasm that had opened between them and the rest of the world. They were bound together by this shared experience, by this unbearable loss, but in that moment, they were also utterly alone. The world outside the sterile walls of the NICU continued, oblivious. Cars drove by, people laughed, life went on. It was a universe that seemed utterly indifferent to the quiet devastation that had just unfolded within these four walls.

"What do we do now?" Kate's voice was barely a whisper, a fragile question lost in the immensity of their sorrow.

Chapter 4

The sterile, fluorescent-lit womb of the hospital had been their reality for weeks. A world of beeping machines and hushed urgency, a universe contained within those four walls. Now, they were home. The car ride had been a silent blur, the muffled sounds of the outside world a distant, alien symphony. Shawn drove, his knuckles white on the steering wheel, his gaze fixed on the ribbon of asphalt unfurling before them. Kate sat beside him, her eyes closed, her face a pale mask of exhaustion and sorrow. The familiar streets of their neighborhood, once a source of comfort, now felt foreign, charged with a terrible significance. Each house, each tree, each familiar landmark was a silent witness to the life they had planned, a life that would never unfold on these streets.

The key turning in the lock of their apartment door was a sound that resonated with an unbearable hollowness. It was the sound of a threshold crossed, not into a shared future, but into a stark, unyielding present. The air inside was still, holding the ghost of anticipation, the faint scent of newness that had been imbued with such fervent hope. It was a hope that now lay shattered, its fragments scattered across the polished hardwood floors. They stood in the entryway, the weight of the silence pressing down on them, heavier than any grief they had yet experienced. It wasn't just an absence of noise; it was the tangible presence of everything that was missing. The unspilled milk, the unread bedtime stories, the unplayed lullabies – they all coalesced into a deafening roar of what would never be.

Hesitantly, they moved deeper into their home, each step an act of wading through a sea of memories. The living room, where they had painstakingly assembled the nursery furniture, now felt vast and empty. The walls, once a canvas for their dreams, seemed to absorb the light, leaving the space feeling dimmer, colder. The sofa, where they had once snuggled, planning every detail of Mae's arrival, now felt like an insurmountable distance between them. Shawn sat down, the cushions sighing beneath his weight, a sound that seemed to mock the stillness he felt within. He stared ahead, his vision unfocused, his mind replaying the sterile white of the hospital room, the phantom weight of Mae in his arms. He felt a profound sense of displacement, as if he had stepped out of his own life and into a strange, echoing void.

Kate, meanwhile, gravitated towards the nursery. It was the epicenter of their shattered dream, the room that held the most potent concentration of their loss. The door, which they had painted a soft, buttery yellow, creaked open, revealing the scene they had so lovingly crafted. The crib, with its freshly ironed sheets and soft bumper pads, stood like a sentinel, a monument to an unfulfilled promise. Beside it, the rocking chair, a cherished find from an antique shop, its wood smooth from years of gentle use, waited for a weight it would never bear. On a small shelf, a collection of plush animals sat in a silent tableau – a floppy-eared bunny, a sleepy bear, a little lamb with a permanently surprised expression. Each one had been chosen with such tenderness, imbued with the hope of future cuddles and whispered secrets. Now, they were simply objects, their softness and warmth rendered meaningless by the absence of the child they were meant to comfort.

Kate walked slowly around the room, her hand trailing along the smooth surface of the crib railing. Her fingers traced the delicate patterns of the bumper pads, the tiny, embroidered stars that had seemed so whimsical just weeks ago. Now, they were sharp reminders of a sky that would remain unobserved by Mae's curious eyes. The small wooden mobile, with its hand-painted moons and clouds, hung motionless, a silent testament to the absence of a cooing infant to watch its gentle sway. She picked up a tiny, hand-knitted cardigan, its wool impossibly soft, the color a delicate rose pink. She held it against her chest, the faint scent of lavender sachet doing little to soothe the ache that radiated from her core.

It was so small, so perfect, a miniature echo of the life she had carried within her. The clothes in the dresser drawers, neatly folded onesies and soft sleepers, were a catalog of a future that would never be. Each garment represented a moment, a milestone, a milestone denied. The yellow duckling bib, the little bear-themed pajamas – they were all rendered poignant and painful by their lack of purpose.

Shawn watched her from the doorway, his heart a heavy stone in his chest. He saw the way her shoulders trembled, the almost imperceptible hitch in her breath. He wanted to go to her, to wrap his arms around her, to share the unbearable weight of their grief. But a strange inertia held him captive. The chasm that had opened between them in the sterile hospital room seemed to have widened, each retreating into the solitary landscape of their own pain. He felt a desperate need for connection, for the solace of shared sorrow, yet the words to bridge the gap eluded him. They were in the same room, breathing the same air, yet they were worlds apart, adrift in the vast ocean of their loss.

He remembered the meticulous care with which they had prepared this room. The hours spent painting, assembling furniture, carefully arranging each item. It had been an act of love, a tangible expression of their burgeoning parenthood. Now, it was a museum of their hopes, a shrine to a life that had flickered and died before it had a chance to truly ignite. The silence in the nursery was profound, a stark contrast to the imagined sounds that had once filled their minds – the gentle gurgles, the soft sighs, the lullabies they had planned to sing. The absence of those sounds was a physical ache, a constant throb that echoed the emptiness in their hearts.

Kate finally turned, her eyes, red-rimmed and glistening, meeting Shawn's. There was a raw vulnerability in her gaze, a plea for understanding that he couldn't quite articulate a response to. She walked towards him, her steps slow, as if moving through treacle. When she reached him, she didn't speak. She simply leaned her head against his chest, her body a trembling silhouette against his. He wrapped his arms around her, holding her tightly, feeling the fragile beat of her heart against his own. It was a small, desperate anchor in the storm.

"It's so quiet," she whispered, her voice muffled against his shirt.

Shawn tightened his embrace. "I know," he murmured, the words catching in his throat. "I know."

Chapter 5

The silence that followed was not comfortable, not peaceful. It was a raw, exposed silence, filled with the unspoken weight of their shared pain. They stood there for a long time, two islands of grief in the quiet expanse of their apartment, finding a fragile solace in the mere physical proximity. It was a beginning, perhaps, a tentative step towards navigating this new, desolate landscape together. But the path ahead felt impossibly long, shrouded in the suffocating stillness that had descended upon their lives. The yellow nursery, once a beacon of hope, was now a constant, heartbreaking reminder of the life that had been, and the profound silence that would now define their days.

Later, much later, when the initial shock had begun to recede, replaced by a dull, pervasive ache, they attempted to resume their lives. Or rather, they attempted to pretend that their lives could continue as before. Shawn tried to focus on work, but the spreadsheets blurred before his eyes, the tasks feeling utterly meaningless. Every email, every phone call, felt like an intrusion from a world that no longer held any relevance for him. The office, a place that had once offered a sense of purpose and accomplishment, now felt like a sterile, alien environment. He found himself staring out the window, his mind drifting back to the empty crib, the still form of his daughter. The mundane demands of his job were a cruel juxtaposition to the magnitude of his loss. He felt disconnected, adrift, unable to find solid ground in the familiar routines of his professional life.

Kate, too, struggled to find any semblance of normalcy. The simple act of going to the grocery store felt like an ordeal. The sight of pregnant women, their faces alight with the joy of anticipation, sent jolts of pain through her. The aisles filled with baby food and tiny clothing were a minefield of memories, each item a fresh stab of grief. She found herself rushing through her errands, desperate to escape the constant reminders of what she had lost. The world outside their apartment continued its relentless march, oblivious to the silent devastation that had consumed their lives. Every laughing child, every happy family, was a painful echo of the life they would never have. She tried to engage in her hobbies, to lose herself in a book or a movie, but her mind always drifted back to the nursery, to the ghost of the daughter she had yearned for. The silence in the apartment was a constant companion, amplifying her sense of isolation.

Even their shared moments felt fraught with an unspoken tension. They would sit in the living room, the television a flickering, meaningless presence, each lost in their own internal world. They would try to talk, to offer words of comfort, but the conversation often faltered, the chasm of their grief too wide to bridge. The shared space between them, once a sanctuary of love and connection, now felt vast and empty. Shawn would reach for Kate's hand, and she would grasp it, but the touch often felt hollow, lacking the warmth and resonance it once held. They were united in their sorrow, yet profoundly alone in their individual experiences of it. The shared trauma had created a bond, but it had also erected barriers, isolating each of them within the fortress of their own pain.

The apartment, once a cozy haven, now felt cavernous and haunted. Every creak of the floorboards, every whisper of the wind outside, seemed to carry the phantom echo of Mae's presence. They would wake in the middle of the night, their hearts pounding, a primal instinct to check on a baby who was no longer there. The empty arms, the silent nursery, were a constant, gnawing reminder of their loss. Sleep offered little respite, often filled with fragmented dreams that left them more exhausted and disoriented than before. The vibrant colors of their future had been leached away, replaced by a monochromatic landscape of grief.

One evening, Shawn found himself standing outside the nursery door, his hand hovering over the knob. He hadn't been able to bring himself to go in there since they had returned home. The memories associated with that room were too sharp, too raw. He finally pushed the door open, the familiar scent of lavender and baby powder hitting him like a physical blow. He walked over to the crib, his gaze fixed on the perfectly made bed. He reached out, his fingers brushing against the soft cotton sheet, imagining the tiny form that should have been nestled there. A single tear traced a path down his cheek, hot and stinging.

Kate appeared in the doorway, her own eyes mirroring his pain. She didn’t say anything, but her presence was a silent acknowledgment of his struggle. She walked over to him, and he turned, pulling her into his arms. They stood there, holding each other, the silence of the nursery enveloping them. It was a silence filled with all the unspoken words, all the unfulfilled dreams, all the love that had been poured into this room and into the daughter they had so desperately wanted.

"We have to... we have to figure out how to live, Shawn," Kate whispered, her voice thick with unshed tears.

Shawn held her tighter, his own resolve hardening. "I know," he said, his voice raspy. "We will. We have to."

But as they stood there, surrounded by the tangible remnants of their shattered dream, the path forward seemed impossibly dark. The apartment, once a symbol of their shared future, now felt like a tomb, a repository of memories that both comforted and tormented them. The silence in their home was a constant, deafening roar, a testament to the profound emptiness that had settled over their lives, and the daunting task of learning to live within its suffocating embrace. The echo of their lost dream seemed to permeate every corner of their lives, a constant, melancholic hum beneath the surface of their forced composure.

They were two souls adrift in a sea of shared grief, the physical distance between them a stark reflection of the emotional chasm that had opened in their hearts, a chasm born from the silent, devastating absence that now defined their existence. The once-familiar walls of their home seemed to press in on them, whispering tales of what might have been, each shadow a reminder of the light that had been extinguished far too soon. The carefully curated innocence of the nursery now felt like a cruel taunt, its softness and warmth a stark contrast to the cold, hard reality of their loss. This was not just the end of a dream; it was the beginning of an era of profound, echoing silence, a silence that would demand their entire being to navigate.

Chapter 6

The silence in their apartment, once a shared space of anticipation and love, had become a battlefield. It wasn't the absence of sound that was so profound, but the palpable weight of unspoken words, of thoughts that circled endlessly within their respective skulls, too heavy to release, too sharp to hold. Kate found herself drawn to the tangible remnants of Mae's too-brief existence, as if by clinging to these physical echoes, she could somehow tether herself to the daughter she had lost. The nursery, a room that had once radiated hope, had become her sanctuary and her prison. She would sit for hours in the rocking chair, the soft fabric cool beneath her fingertips, Mae's tiny lavender-scented cardigan clutched in her hand. She'd trace the delicate stitches, the impossibly small buttons, each detail a testament to a future that would never unfold. Sometimes, she'd pick up one of the plush animals – the sleepy bear, the floppy-eared bunny – and hold it close, imagining Mae's small hand clutching its fur, a phantom warmth against her own skin.

These were not acts of morbid obsession, but of desperate preservation. In these objects, she found a semblance of connection, a way to keep Mae's memory alive in a world that seemed intent on erasing her. She would whisper to the cardigan, to the bear, recounting imagined stories, sharing the quiet moments of her day, as if Mae were simply asleep in the next room. The world outside their apartment continued its relentless hum, but within these four walls, time had fractured, and Kate was suspended in the amber of her grief, meticulously tending to the fragile memories.

Shawn, on the other hand, experienced his grief as a suffocating shroud, an all-encompassing darkness that stole his breath and leached the color from his world. The tangible felt alien, even cruel. The baby clothes, the perfectly assembled crib, seemed to mock him with their silent testament to what should have been. He couldn't bear to enter the nursery, the room a visceral reminder of a future that had been stolen before it had even begun. His withdrawal was a desperate act of self-preservation, a futile attempt to outrun the crushing weight of despair. He found solace, or rather, a temporary reprieve, in the monotony of routine. He buried himself in his work, not out of any newfound passion, but as a means of anaesthetizing his senses. The sterile environment of his office, the predictable rhythm of tasks, offered a fragile bulwark against the relentless tide of his emotions. He would stare at his computer screen, the words blurring into an indistinguishable mess, his mind a thousand miles away, lost in the echoing silence of their apartment.

He yearned for connection, for the comfort of Kate's presence, but the chasm that had opened between them felt too vast to cross. He saw her retreating into her own world of mementes, and he felt a pang of alienation. He believed, with a certainty that gnawed at him, that she couldn't possibly understand the depth of his own desolation. His grief was a gaping wound, raw and exposed, and he felt a primal urge to shield himself from anything that might cause it further pain. He saw her holding the cardigan, and he felt a surge of something akin to resentment, a bitter envy of her ability to find comfort in such fragile things. He, however, found himself adrift in a sea of abstract pain, an emptiness so profound it threatened to swallow him whole.

Their evenings together became a silent ballet of avoidancc. They would sit at the dining table, the meticulously prepared meals – often something Shawn had picked up on his way home, a concession to the dwindling energy Kate possessed – growing cold between them. The clinking of silverware against porcelain seemed unnervingly loud in the suffocating stillness. Shawn would pick at his food, his gaze fixed on some distant point on the wall, his mind a tangled knot of unspoken thoughts. Kate would push her food around her plate, her appetite long gone, her focus solely on the gnawing ache in her chest. They would try to engage in conversation, tentative probes into each other's day, but the words often died on their lips, dissolving into the heavy air.

"How was work?" Kate might venture, her voice a fragile thread.

Shawn would offer a monosyllabic response, "Fine." Or, "Busy." The truth, that his work felt meaningless, that his mind was a constant replay of their loss, was too much to articulate. He'd look at Kate, her face pale and drawn, her eyes shadowed with a grief that mirrored his own, yet felt so utterly different. He believed she couldn't comprehend the all-consuming nature of his despair, the way it had hollowed him out from the inside. He saw her ritual with the objects, and a part of him felt shut out, excluded from her process of mourning. He couldn't find solace in the physical; his pain was an abstract, crushing weight that demanded a solitary reckoning.

"Did you... did you go into the nursery today?" he might ask, his voice barely a whisper, a desperate attempt to breach the wall between them.

Kate's breath would catch, and she'd shake her head, her gaze falling to her plate. "Just sat for a bit," she'd murmur, her voice thick with unshed tears. She would avoid his eyes, afraid he'd see the depth of her sorrow, afraid he'd dismiss her comfort-seeking as weakness. She believed, with an equal and opposite certainty, that Shawn was retreating from her, that he found her grief somehow unbearable. She couldn't understand his detachment from Mae's things, his inability to even speak her name with any regularity. To her, these objects were Mae's legacy, the only tangible proof that their daughter had existed. His apparent indifference felt like a betrayal, a subtle erasure of their shared love. She longed for him to hold her, to weep with her, to share the unbearable weight of their loss, but his silence, his stoic withdrawal, felt like a wall he was deliberately constructing between them.

Their evenings would often end with them retreating to separate parts of the apartment. Shawn would find himself in the living room, the television a flickering, meaningless distraction, his mind replaying the sterile white of the hospital room, the doctor's somber words. He'd stare at the blank wall, the silence amplifying the hollowness within him. Kate, meanwhile, would retreat to their bedroom, often finding herself in the dark, the soft glow of a nightlight the only illumination. She'd lie in bed, Mae's tiny cardigan folded on her nightstand, a silent sentinel, and replay the memories, clinging to the phantom sensation of Mae kicking within her. She'd listen for Shawn's movements, for the sound of him getting a glass of water, for any sign that he was still present in their shared space. But often, he remained a phantom presence, his grief a barrier that kept them physically together, yet emotionally miles apart.

The subtle cracks in their marriage, once hairline fractures barely visible beneath the surface of their shared happiness, were widening into gaping chasms. They were two ships passing in the night, each lost in their own tempest, unable to see the distress signals of the other. Shawn would catch himself watching Kate, her quiet rituals, her withdrawn demeanor, and a flicker of something akin to frustration would ignite within him. He'd interpret her quiet reflection as a lack of understanding of his own internal torment. He believed she was trapped in a world of tangible sorrow, unable to grasp the abstract, all-consuming void that had become his reality. He would try to reach out, a hand on her shoulder, a hesitant question, but his words, when they came, felt clumsy, inadequate. He was acutely aware of the distance that had opened between them, and the more he tried to bridge it, the more it seemed to stretch.

Chapter 7

"Are you alright?" he'd ask, his voice gruff, a poor substitute for the tenderness he felt but couldn't express.

Kate would flinch slightly at his touch, her body tensing before relaxing into a semblance of acceptance. "I'm okay," she'd reply, the lie tasting bitter on her tongue. She couldn't articulate the raw ache that consumed her, the constant phantom limb sensation of Mae's absence. She'd look at Shawn, his own eyes holding a pain she recognized, yet somehow felt distinct from her own. She longed for him to acknowledge the depth of her loss, to validate her grief in a way that his stoicism seemed to deny. She'd find herself watching him with a mixture of longing and resentment, wondering if he would ever truly understand the visceral nature of her pain, the way it was woven into the very fabric of her being. The objects in the nursery were her anchors, her proof of existence, and his disengagement from them felt like a personal indictment.

One evening, as they sat in the quiet, suffocating expanse of the living room, the television casting a pale, flickering light across their faces, Shawn finally broke the silence. It wasn't a conscious decision, but a desperate urge to shatter the oppressive stillness that had become their constant companion.

"I don't know how to do this, Kate," he said, his voice a raw whisper, devoid of its usual strength. He wasn't looking at her, his gaze fixed on the dark rectangle of the television screen, as if searching for answers in its blank depths. "I don't know how to live like this."

Kate turned her head slowly, her eyes meeting his. There was a raw vulnerability in his admission, a crack in the stoic facade she had come to expect. For a fleeting moment, a surge of hope – a dangerous, fragile thing – flickered within her. Perhaps this was it, the moment they could finally connect, finally begin to heal together.

"I know," she replied, her voice trembling. "Me neither." She wanted to reach for him, to pull him close, to offer the comfort she so desperately craved herself. But the habit of isolation, of retreating into her own internal landscape, held her captive. The words she wanted to say – *I miss her so much, Shawn. It hurts so much. Are you hurting too? Tell me you're hurting* – remain locked behind her teeth.

Shawn let out a shaky breath, a sound that seemed to carry the weight of years of unspoken sorrow. He couldn't bring himself to articulate the suffocating despair that had enveloped him, the feeling of being adrift in an endless ocean of grief. He couldn't explain why the nursery felt like a tomb, why the tangible reminders of Mae were a source of such profound agony. He believed, with a conviction that chilled him to the bone, that Kate's grief, while immense, was different. Hers was rooted in the tangible, in the objects she could hold, the memories she could revisit. His was a void, an abstract torment that defied articulation, a crushing weight that left him breathless and numb. He saw her clutching the cardigan, and he felt a pang of envy, a desperate longing for a tangible anchor in his own sea of desolation.

"It's just... too quiet," he finally managed to say, the words a meager offering. "Everything is too quiet."

Kate nodded, a single tear tracing a path down her cheek. "Yes," she whispered, her voice thick. "It is." She understood his words on a primal level, the deafening silence that had descended upon their lives. But she also felt a disconnect. Her quiet was filled with Mae's phantom presence, with the rustle of tiny clothes, the imagined coos and sighs. His quiet, she suspected, was a hollow echo, an emptiness that mirrored the void he felt within himself.

The conversation, like so many others, faltered and died. The fragile bridge they had momentarily built had crumbled, leaving them once again on separate shores. They were bound together by their shared loss, yet isolated by the unique and profound ways they experienced it. The carefully constructed routines, the forced attempts at normalcy, were becoming increasingly strained. The subtle shifts in their behavior, the growing emotional distance, were not a sign of a lack of love, but a testament to the overwhelming power of their individual grief. They were two souls adrift, each navigating their own storm, and the silent, suffocating space between them was growing larger with each passing, agonizing day. The comfortable intimacy they had once shared was being eroded, replaced by a tense, unspoken distance that threatened to unravel the very fabric of their marriage, leaving them stranded in the desolate landscape of their individual sorrows.

Chapter 8

The silence that had settled over Shawn's life after Mae's death had been a profound, suffocating thing. It was the silence of absence, of a future unwritten, of a love that had no outlet. But the silence that descended after his father's death was a different beast altogether. It was a deafening roar, a gaping wound in the very fabric of his reality, echoing with the stark, brutal finality of a choice made in desperation. John. His father. The man who had always seemed an immovable pillar, a constant in Shawn's turbulent existence, was gone. Not faded, not weakened, but *gone*, in a way that defied comprehension, a violent severance from the world, from *him*.

The phone call came on a Tuesday, a mundane day shattered by the chilling voice of Uncle Roger. John. Shawn's father. Dead. Suicide. The words were a brutal echo in the silence of the apartment, a shockwave that rippled through Shawn's already fractured world. John, a man of quiet disposition, a man who had never harbored anger, had succumbed to a pain Shawn had never truly understood.

This wasn't a gentle slipping away. This was a violent tearing. He saw his father's face, not as it was in recent years, etched with a weariness Shawn now recognized as a deep, unspoken sorrow, but as it had been in his childhood – strong, capable, a shield against the world. How could that man, that image, have arrived at such an end? It was a question that clawed at him, a relentless phantom limb of a father-son relationship that felt irrevocably broken, not just by death, but by the manner of it.

And then, just as the shock of John's death began to solidify into a dull, persistent ache, came the news of William. His grandfather. The patriarch, the keeper of stories, the man whose quiet presence had always offered a sense of continuity, a link to a past Shawn had only glimpsed. William, who had weathered so many storms, who had carried the weight of generations, had succumbed to illness. The timing was a cruel, cosmic joke. Two men, anchors in Shawn's life, vanishing within months of each other, leaving behind a void so immense it threatened to swallow him whole. It wasn't just grief; it was an unraveling, a profound disorientation. The familiar landscape of his life had been violently rearranged, leaving him stranded in a desolate wilderness.

He found himself staring at the walls of his apartment, the same walls that had once held the gentle anticipation of Mae's arrival, now echoing with the hollow thud of these new losses. The grief from Mae's death had been a sharp, immediate pain, a wound that had bled him dry. This new grief, however, was a slow poison, seeping into his bones, contaminating every thought, every memory. It was compounded, layered, a grotesque accumulation of sorrow that left him feeling hollowed out, a mere shell animated by a desperate, primal urge to simply survive the next breath.

The concept of legacy, once a distant notion whispered in hushed tones about great artists or historical figures, now pressed down on him with an unbearable weight. What was his father's legacy? A life that ended in such profound despair? And his grandfather's? A history of stoicism, of quiet endurance, that now felt like a mere prelude to an inevitable decline? Shawn felt trapped in a narrative he hadn't chosen, a story of loss and abandonment that seemed to be written into his very DNA. He'd always been aware of a certain melancholy that clung to his father, a shadow that even his attempts at joviality couldn't entirely dispel. Now, in the brutal clarity of hindsight, he saw the signs, the subtle cracks in the facade that he had, in his youth, dismissed as mere personality quirks. His father's increasingly erratic behavior, the hushed phone calls, the periods of withdrawal – they weren't just stress. They were cries for help, lost in the cacophony of everyday life.

This compounding grief was doing something insidious to Shawn's perception of the world. The existential dread that had been a low hum beneath the surface of his life, amplified by Mae's death, now roared to life. He began to see death not as a distant inevitability, but as an ever-present specter, lurking in the shadows of every moment. Life felt fragile, arbitrary, a precarious dance on the edge of an abyss. The mundane activities that had once provided structure – his work, his routines – now felt futile, like rearranging deck chairs on a sinking ship. What was the point of striving, of building, of loving, when the ultimate end was so stark, so absolute?

He found himself consumed by a profound sense of abandonment. First Mae, his child, his future, ripped away. Then his father chose to leave. Then his grandfather, his link to the past, fading away. Each loss was a confirmation of a fundamental loneliness, a deep-seated belief that he was destined to be left behind, to navigate this fractured world alone. The world, once a place of possibility, now seemed like a cruel, indifferent stage on which he was forced to play out a tragedy.

Kate, too, was a reminder of the chasm that now separated him from the life they had once shared. Her grief, though deeply felt, was a tangible thing, rooted in the physical absence of Mae. She clung to the objects, to the memories, finding a painful solace in their very existence. Shawn envied her this ability, this concrete connection to their lost daughter. His own grief was formless, a suffocating fog that distorted his vision, that stole his breath. He saw her sitting in the nursery, holding Mae's tiny cardigan, and he felt a surge of a pain so acute it was almost physical. It was the pain of exclusion, of being unable to share even the most profound sorrow, because his experience of it was so fundamentally different, so isolated. He felt a desperate need for her to understand the all-consuming nature of his despair, the way it had hollowed him out, leaving him adrift in a sea of existential questions. But how could he articulate the crushing weight of his father's suicide, the inherited darkness he now felt coursing through his veins, to a woman who was still grappling with the silent tragedy of their lost child?

He started to revisit old family photographs, the glossy squares of captured moments now imbued with a chilling irony. There was his father, younger, smiling, a man who seemed to hold the world in his hands. There was his grandfather, a stoic figure even in his youth, a testament to endurance. And there were younger versions of himself, a child who believed in the inherent goodness of things, who hadn't yet tasted the bitter draught of irreversible loss. He looked at these images, searching for clues, for a pattern, for anything that might explain the darkness that seemed to have claimed his father, and now threatened to consume him. He saw the subtle tensions in his parents' smiles, the unspoken weariness in his father's eyes even in happier times, and he realized that the veneer of normalcy had always been thin. His family history, he suspected, was not a simple narrative of love and support, but a complex tapestry woven with threads of unspoken pain, of inherited anxieties, of a predisposition to melancholy that had finally manifested in its most tragic form.

The weight of this inherited despair was suffocating. It wasn't just his father's pain he carried, but a lineage of it. He felt the ghosts of his ancestors, their unspoken sorrows, their quiet battles, all converging within him. He imagined his father, in his final moments, perhaps seeing himself as a release, a way to break free from the cycle of suffering that he believed was his destiny. And that, Shawn realized with a chilling certainty, was the most terrifying legacy of all: the belief that suffering was inevitable, that death was the only true escape.

He started to question everything he had ever believed about purpose, about meaning, about love. If his father, a man he had loved and admired, could succumb to such despair, what hope was there for anyone? If life was so fragile, so easily extinguished, what was the point of all the struggle, all the striving? He looked at Kate, her quiet strength a beacon in the darkness, and a part of him longed to share his newfound, terrifying understanding of the world. But he also knew, with a certainty that chilled him, that she was not ready for it. Her grief, though immense, was still rooted in love, in memory, in the tangible. His was a plunge into the abyss, a confrontation with the void.

The legacy of his father's death wasn't just the sorrow it left behind, but the questions it forced Shawn to confront. Questions about his own capacity for despair, about the darkness that lurked within his own family history, about the very meaning of existence. He was no longer just a grieving son, a grieving husband, a grieving father. He was a man standing at the precipice of an existential crisis, haunted by the specter of his father's choice, and grappling with the terrifying realization that the darkness he saw in his father might also reside within himself. The silence of Mae's nursery had been a silence of absence. The silence now echoing through Shawn's life was a silence of dread, a deafening roar of unanswered questions, of a future shrouded in an impenetrable darkness. He was no longer just mourning a loss; he was wrestling with the very foundations of his being, and the outcome of that battle remained terrifyingly uncertain. The weight of his legacy, both personal and ancestral, was an almost unbearable burden, pressing down on him, threatening to crush him entirely. He felt like a man adrift in a storm, the lightning illuminating brief, terrifying glimpses of a future he was not sure he wanted to face, a future where the specter of death and despair seemed to be his only true inheritance. He looked at his hands, the same hands his father had possessed, and he wondered, with a cold dread, if they too were capable of writing such a devastating final chapter.

Chapter 9

The edifice of Shawn's existence, once sturdy enough to withstand the tremors of Mae's death, was now crumbling from within, the twin blows of his father's and grandfather's deaths acting as a relentless battering ram against its very foundations. The professional sphere, which had always served as a semblance of order in his life, a place where tangible achievements could momentarily push back the encroaching shadows, began to buckle under the immense pressure. His work, once a source of focus and even pride, became an impossible mountain to scale. The meticulous attention to detail that had defined his career, the ability to dissect complex problems and forge solutions, was now utterly beyond his grasp. His mind, a battlefield of grief and existential dread, could no longer find the quiet space required for concentration.

Each email that pinged in his inbox, each request that landed on his desk, felt like another stone dislodged from the already precarious walls of his mental fortitude. He would stare at spreadsheets, the columns and rows blurring into an indistinguishable morass of numbers and symbols, his thoughts inevitably drifting to the sterile quiet of the morgue, the hollow echo of the detective's voice, the phantom sensation of his grandfather's frail hand in his. The pervasive anxiety that had been a low hum since his father's passing now escalated into a roaring torrent, drowning out any rational thought. Depression, a familiar if unwelcome guest since Mae's death, returned with a vengeance, not as a subtle melancholy, but as an all-consuming inertia, a leaden cloak that rendered even the simplest tasks Herculean.

He'd sit at his desk, the fluorescent lights of the office casting a sterile glow on his slumped shoulders, and find himself utterly paralyzed. The urgent deadlines, the demanding clients, the very rhythm of the workday – all of it seemed to exist in a separate reality, a world he could no longer inhabit. He'd try to force himself, to engage, to articulate a coherent thought, but the words would catch in his throat, strangled by the sheer weight of his sorrow. He'd spend hours staring out the window, the cityscape a blur of indifferent buildings, his mind replaying fragmented memories: his father's strained smile, his grandfather's stoic silence, the empty cradle in the nursery. The present was a torment, the past a haunted landscape, and the future an unfathomable void.

The inevitable summons to his manager's office felt less like a shock and more like a grim confirmation of what he already knew. The conversation was a blur of platitudes and corporate jargon, of "performance issues" and "unsustainable trajectory." Shawn sat there, numb, the words washing over him without penetrating the dense fog of his grief. He didn't argue, didn't plead. He understood. He had, in essence, already fired himself, every waking moment dedicated to the unraveling of his professional self. When the finality of it settled, the words "redundant" and "severance package" echoing in the sterile room, a strange, almost perverse sense of relief washed over him. Another anchor, however ill-fitting it had become, had been cut loose.

Losing his job was more than just a professional setback; it was the stripping away of another vital layer of his identity. He was no longer Shawn, the promising architect, the meticulous project manager. He was simply Shawn, the grieving man, adrift without the structure and purpose that his career had provided. The loss of routine was profound. The alarm clock that used to jolt him into a structured day was silenced. The commute, once a tedious but predictable part of his existence, was no longer a necessity. He found himself waking late, the dawn light filtering through his blinds, a stark reminder of the hours he had lost, the potential he had squandered.

The days stretched out before him, vast and empty. He would wander through his apartment, the silence of the rooms amplifying his isolation. He'd find himself standing in the doorway of Mae's nursery, a room that had once represented hope and anticipation, now a shrine to what might have been, and a stark symbol of his current despair. He'd touch the soft fabrics of her untouched clothes, the scent of lavender and baby powder, a phantom perfume that choked him. These were memories he could not share with Kate, not truly. Her grief, though profound, was tethered to the tangible absence of their daughter. His was a more pervasive, existential anguish, a grief that encompassed not only Mae but the dissolution of his father, the passing of his grandfather, and the shattering of his own sense of self.

The inertia was a physical force, pinning him to his sofa, to his bed. He'd spend hours simply existing, the television flickering in the background, a mindless drone that provided a temporary distraction from the gnawing emptiness. He'd lose track of time, the day dissolving into night, marked only by the changing patterns of light outside his window. He found himself withdrawing further, both from Kate and from the outside world. The effort of conversation, of maintaining even a superficial connection, felt exhausting. He was trapped in a labyrinth of his own grief, unable to find the exit, increasingly convinced that there was no exit to be found.

He'd revisit the photographs, the digital albums that chronicled a life that now seemed impossibly distant. There were images of his father, laughing, his eyes crinkling at the corners, a warmth that Shawn now recognized as a carefully guarded ember against a deep-seated cold. There were pictures of his grandfather, his face a roadmap of a life lived with quiet resilience, a man who had witnessed so much and spoken so little of it. And there were photos of himself, younger, vibrant, before the weight of loss had begun to settle on his shoulders. He searched these images for clues, for answers, for a roadmap that might lead him back to some semblance of himself. But the past, as he now understood it, was not a reliable guide. It was a collection of curated moments, a fragile veneer over a more complex, often darker, reality.

He found himself increasingly drawn to the periphery, to the liminal spaces of life. He'd spend hours in parks, not engaging with anyone, just observing the ebb and flow of human activity from a distance. He'd watch families laughing, couples strolling hand-in-hand, children playing with an unburdened joy, and feel an ache so profound it was almost physical. These were the scenes he had once been a part of, the life he had once known. Now, they felt like a foreign country, its customs and language lost to him.

The silence of his apartment became a character in itself, a constant, oppressive presence. It amplified the echo of his own thoughts, the relentless rhythm of his grief. He'd try to fill it with music, with podcasts, with anything that offered a distraction, but the silence always seemed to seep back in, a persistent tide that threatened to drown him. It was a silence born of absence, but also of a profound, suffocating loneliness. It was the sound of his own unraveling.

Chapter 10

The gnawing emptiness within him, a void carved by loss and magnified by unemployment, became an insistent, unbearable ache. His apartment, once a sanctuary, now felt like a tomb, its silence amplifying the cacophony of his own despair. Sleep offered no solace, only a temporary deferral of consciousness, a brief respite before the relentless onslaught of memory and regret would drag him back to the surface. He'd awaken in the predawn stillness, the ghosts of his father, his grandfather, and Mae swirling in the dim light, their spectral presence a constant, suffocating reminder of all that had been irrevocably lost. He'd lie there, a prisoner of his own mind, the weight of his existence pressing down on him with an almost physical force.

It was in this state of profound emotional desolation that he first reached for the bottle. It wasn't a conscious decision, not at first. It was more of an instinctual reach, a desperate attempt to quell the internal storm that threatened to consume him. He'd found a half-empty bottle of whiskey tucked away in the back of a cupboard, a forgotten relic from a time when social gatherings, however infrequent, had necessitated such provisions. He uncorked it, the sharp, medicinal scent a familiar, almost comforting, aroma. He poured a generous measure into a tumbler, the amber liquid catching the scant light. He hesitated for a fraction of a second, a flicker of self-awareness, a tiny spark in the encroaching darkness. But the ache, the relentless pressure, was too great. He raised the glass to his lips and drank.

The effect was immediate, a warm tide that spread through his chest, dulling the sharp edges of his pain. It was a temporary reprieve, a brief ceasefire in the war raging within him. The relentless loop of anxieties, the crushing weight of grief, the suffocating sense of failure – they all receded, their power diminished by the encroaching fog. He poured another drink, then another. Each swallow was a small act of surrender, a conscious decision to seek oblivion, however fleeting. He wasn't looking for answers, or for strength. He was simply looking for an escape. And in the numbing embrace of the alcohol, he found it.

The next morning was a blur of regret and physical discomfort. His head throbbed, his mouth was dry, and a vague sense of unease lingered in the pit of his stomach. He remembered the previous night, the frantic pursuit of numbness, the growing desperation. He chastened himself, a familiar internal monologue of self-recrimination. He wouldn't let it happen again. He knew, intellectually, that this was not a solution. It was a temporary anesthetic, and the pain would return, sharper and more potent, once the effects wore off. Yet, as the day wore on, and the familiar specter of his grief began to reassert itself, the siren song of the bottle grew louder, more insistent.

He found himself seeking out reasons to drink. A particularly difficult memory would surface, a pang of guilt would gnaw at him, a wave of despair would threaten to overwhelm him – and he would reach for the whiskey. He began to rationalize his behavior. It was just a way to cope, he told himself. It was a temporary crutch. He wasn't an alcoholic; he was a man in mourning, a man who had suffered unimaginable losses. He was simply taking a moment for himself, a necessary indulgence to weather the storm.

The routine began to establish itself, insidiously at first, then with a frightening regularity. Mornings were spent battling the hangover and the guilt. Afternoons were a haze of low-grade anxiety, punctuated by the furtive anticipation of the evening. Evenings were dedicated to the bottle.

He'd sit in his living room, the curtains drawn, the only illumination coming from the flickering screen of the television, its mindless chatter a distant hum. He'd pour himself a drink, then another, slowly surrendering to the familiar warmth, the welcome numbness. He'd lose track of time, the hours dissolving into a hazy, alcohol-induced stupor.

Kate, his wife, began to notice the changes. At first, she attributed his withdrawn nature and his increased absences from their shared life to his grief and job loss. She was grieving too, and she understood the profound impact of their losses. She'd try to reach him, to engage him in conversation, to draw him out of his shell. But he'd deflect her questions, offer vague reassurances, or retreat into a sullen silence. He was building a wall around himself, brick by brick, and alcohol was the mortar that cemented it into place.

Their conversations, once filled with shared hopes and intimate reflections, became strained and superficial. He'd flinch at her questions, become defensive when she expressed concern, and often resort to outright evasion. "I'm just tired, Kate," he'd say, his voice flat. "Just need some time to myself." But the time he needed was increasingly being spent in the solitary company of a bottle. He'd promise her he'd cut back, he'd promise her he'd stop, but the promises were as empty as the bottles he'd discard.

One evening, Kate confronted him directly. She found him slumped in his armchair, a half-empty bottle on the side table, his eyes glazed and unfocused. The scene was a stark indictment of his current state, a tangible manifestation of the chasm that had opened between them.

"Shawn, we need to talk," she said, her voice quiet but firm.

He looked at her, a flicker of recognition in his eyes, quickly followed by a wave of shame. He tried to form a coherent response, but the words wouldn't come. He simply shrugged, a gesture of weary resignation.

“This isn’t you, Shawn,” she continued, her voice cracking with emotion. “This... this drinking... it’s not helping. It’s making things worse. You’re shutting me out. You’re shutting yourself in.”

He finally found his voice, though it was thick and slurred. “I’m just... trying to get by, Kate. It’s hard. You don’t understand how hard it is.”

“I do understand!” she cried, tears welling in her eyes. “I’m grieving too, Shawn! But I’m not drowning myself in alcohol. I’m trying to... to survive this. Together. But you’re not here. You’re somewhere else, with that bottle.”

He recoiled from her words, the accusation stinging him. He wanted to defend himself, to explain the unbearable pain, the suffocating darkness, but the words felt hollow, inadequate. He simply shook his head, a futile attempt to deny the reality she was laying bare.

“I can’t do this, Shawn,” she whispered, her voice barely audible. “I can’t watch you do this to yourself. To us.”

She turned and walked out of the room, leaving him alone with his shame and the silent, accusing presence of the bottle. The encounter left him with a crushing weight of guilt, but it didn’t break his reliance on alcohol. Instead, it seemed to solidify his resolve to continue his descent, to seek solace in the very thing that was destroying him. He told himself that Kate didn’t understand, that she couldn’t possibly comprehend the depths of his despair. He clung to this narrative, a self-serving justification that allowed him to maintain his destructive habit.

The moments of clarity, when they came, were the most agonizing. He’d wake up in the middle of the night, sober enough to see the mess he was making of his life, the damage he was inflicting on Kate, the precipice he was teetering on. He’d feel a surge of panic, a desperate urge to pull himself back from the brink. He'd vow to stop, to change, to seek help. He'd even, on occasion, pour the remaining alcohol down the drain, a symbolic act of renunciation.

His work life, the one arena where he had once found a semblance of control and purpose, had already imploded. Now, his personal life was beginning to unravel at an equally alarming pace. The strain on his marriage was palpable. Kate, though she loved him, was growing increasingly weary. She was caught between her love for the man he had been and the stranger he was becoming. She tried to be supportive, to offer him a lifeline, but he seemed determined to pull away, to drag her down with him.

He began to avoid social situations altogether. The thought of facing friends, of having to explain his absence from work, his gaunt appearance, his erratic behavior, filled him with a paralyzing dread. He'd make excuses, cancel plans at the last minute, or simply stop answering his phone. He was isolating himself, not just from the world, but from the people who cared about him, the people who might have been able to pull him back from the edge.

The bottle became his sole companion, his confidante, his only escape. It was a treacherous embrace, a false comfort that offered fleeting oblivion at the cost of his health, his relationships, and his very sense of self. He was caught in its snare, a prisoner of his own making, the darkness deepening with each passing day, each swallowed drink. He was adrift, a ship slowly sinking beneath the waves, the bottle a life raft that was itself waterlogged and doomed. The path forward, once a series of clear choices and defined steps, had dissolved into a murky, alcohol-fueled haze, and he could no longer see the way back to shore. The silence of his apartment was no longer just empty; it was filled with the clinking of ice, the pour of amber liquid, the quiet, steady sound of his own disintegration.

Chapter 11

The silence between them had become a tangible thing, a heavy shroud draped over the ruins of their shared life. It wasn't the comfortable silence of intimacy, the kind that allows souls to converse without words. This was a fractured silence, brittle and sharp, capable of shattering at the slightest provocation. Kate would watch Shawn across the dinner table, the clink of his fork against his plate a percussive punctuation to the vast, echoing emptiness that had swallowed their conversations whole. He'd offer a monosyllabic response to her questions, a mumbled "fine" or a dismissive "I'm tired," and the gulf between them would widen, a chasm carved by unspoken resentments and unmet needs.

She remembered the easy laughter that had once flowed between them, the shared jokes that only they understood, the comfortable rhythm of their everyday discourse. Now, each utterance felt loaded, fraught with the potential for misunderstanding. When she'd tentatively ask about his day, her voice laced with a fragile hope, he'd offer a clipped, factual account, devoid of any personal reflection, as if recounting the weather to a stranger. His eyes, once so full of warmth and recognition for her, now often seemed distant, veiled by a haze that had nothing to do with exhaustion and everything to do with the bottle he increasingly turned to.

The absence of Mae, a wound that had never truly healed, seemed to have metastasized, infecting every corner of their relationship. The shared grief, which she had hoped would forge them into something stronger, had instead become a wedge, driving them apart. Each of them grieved in their own way, and their methods were increasingly incompatible. While Kate sought connection, a desperate need to share the burden and find solace in each other's arms, Shawn retreated, building walls of silence and self-medication around himself. She craved validation for her pain, a simple acknowledgment of the devastation they had both endured. But Shawn, lost in his own internal fog, seemed incapable of offering it, his own pain a consuming inferno that left no room for anyone else's.

The anniversaries, once milestones celebrated with shared joy and quiet reflection, had become poignant reminders of their fracturing connection. Their wedding anniversary had passed with barely a mention. Shawn had been withdrawn all day, his gaze fixed on some unseen point beyond the walls of their apartment. Kate had tried, her heart aching with a desperate longing for the man she had married. She'd prepared his favorite meal, lit candles, and put on the music they'd danced to on their wedding night. But he'd barely touched the food, his attention a million miles away, and the music had simply underscored the deafening silence between them. He'd offered a perfunctory "Happy anniversary, Kate" as he excused himself early, the words tasting like ash in his mouth. She'd spent the evening alone, surrounded by the ghosts of happier times, the unlit candles a testament to their failed celebration.

Their intimacy, the bedrock of their marriage, had eroded to a point where it felt like a distant memory. The physical touch that had once been a natural expression of their love had become awkward, strained. A hand held a moment too long felt like a burden, a kiss on the cheek, a perfunctory gesture. He seemed to flinch away from her touch, not out of aversion, but out of a profound disconnect, as if her presence, her very realness, was an intrusion into the hazy world he inhabited. She missed the way he used to pull her close, the way their bodies fit together as if they were made for each other. Now, the space between them felt vast and unbridgeable, even in the confines of their bedroom.

She tried to talk to him about Mae, about the gaping hole her absence had left in her life, about the dreams they had shared for their daughter. But Shawn would become visibly uncomfortable, his gaze shifting, his jaw tightening. It was as if the very mention of Mae's name was a painful reminder of everything he felt he had failed to protect, to cherish, to hold onto. He couldn't bear to revisit the past, to confront the depth of his loss, and so he shut down, leaving Kate to navigate her grief in solitude. She longed to share her memories of Mae, to talk about her quirks, her laughter, her unique spirit, but Shawn had erected an impenetrable barrier around those memories, leaving her to hold them alone.

The feeling of being utterly alone within her marriage was a pervasive, soul-crushing ache. She was living with a man who was physically present but emotionally absent. He was a ghost in their shared home, a spectral presence haunting the spaces where their life used to be. She felt invisible, unheard, her needs and feelings relegated to a secondary, if not entirely forgotten, status. She would find herself speaking aloud to an empty room, her words echoing back to her, a hollow testament to her isolation. She longed for a simple conversation, a shared moment of understanding, a hand to hold that felt like it belonged to the man she loved.

She remembered a specific incident, a heated exchange over something trivial - a misplaced set of keys, perhaps - that had escalated into a full-blown argument. In the heat of the moment, Shawn had accused her of not understanding his pain, of being selfish, of not appreciating what he had lost. The words had landed like a physical blow. "Don't you dare tell me I don't understand loss, Shawn!" she had retorted, her voice a raw scream. "I lost our daughter! I lost the life we were building! And I am losing you, too!" The raw honesty of her words hung in the air, heavy with unspoken grief. Shawn had flinched, a look of profound pain flashing across his face before it was quickly masked by a stony indifference. He had then turned and walked away, leaving her sobbing in the middle of the living room, the silence once again reclaiming its dominion.

Kate found herself withdrawing, not out of a desire to hurt Shawn, but out of a desperate need for self-preservation. She began to focus on other aspects of her life, finding solace in her work, in the quiet companionship of her few remaining friends. She learned to occupy herself, to fill the void left by Shawn's emotional absence with her own activities, her own interests. But even in these moments of relative peace, the underlying ache of loneliness persisted, a dull throb beneath the surface of her carefully constructed composure.

She tried to understand his struggle, to empathize with the weight of his grief and his perceived failures. She knew he was hurting, deeply and profoundly. But his method of coping, his descent into alcoholism, felt like a betrayal. It felt like he was actively choosing to push her away, to drown their shared life in a sea of liquor. She longed to reach him, to pull him back to shore, but he seemed determined to swim further out, towards a horizon she couldn't see, a place she couldn't follow.

The shared intimacy they had once known had been replaced by a tense politeness, a careful navigation of treacherous emotional waters. They were no longer partners, lovers, confidantes. They were two strangers sharing a house, bound by habit and the lingering echoes of a love that was slowly, painfully, fading. The loss of Mae had been a devastating blow, but the subsequent loss of their connection, the erosion of their marriage, felt like a slow, agonizing amputation. Each fractured silence, each unanswered question, each missed anniversary, was another cut, another piece of their shared life that was being irrevocably lost. They were living in the aftermath of a storm, the landscape of their marriage irrevocably altered, the paths they once walked together now diverging into separate, lonely territories.

Chapter 12

The air in their apartment had become thick, not just with the stale scent of days lived in isolation, but with an almost palpable weight of unspoken words. Kate felt it pressing in on her, a constant reminder of the silence that had become their unwanted third companion. Shawn, a silhouette against the dim light filtering through the blinds, was a familiar stranger. He sat at the kitchen table, his shoulders slumped, a mug of coffee growing cold in his hands. She watched him, her heart a familiar ache in her chest, a dull thrum against the ribs that felt increasingly hollow. The chasm between them, a silent, gaping wound, seemed to widen with each passing hour, each shared breath that went unacknowledged. She yearned for a bridge, a fragile thread to weave between their separate islands of grief.

It was in this atmosphere of quiet desperation, a moment suspended between resignation and a flicker of defiant hope, that Kate's idea began to take root. It wasn't a sudden revelation, but a slow blossoming, nurtured by the fertile soil of her longing for connection, for a shared purpose in the face of overwhelming loss. The emptiness in their lives, the gaping hole left by Mae's absence, felt like a vast, uncultivated field. What if, she mused, they could coax something beautiful from that barren landscape? What if they could plant a seed, a living testament to the love that still pulsed, however faintly, beneath the layers of their pain?

The thought, once formed, began to gather momentum, a tiny snowball rolling down a slope. It was an act of defiance against the inertia that had seized them, a gentle push against the immovable wall of their despair. She envisioned a place, a tangible space, where Mae's memory could bloom, not as a somber reminder of what was lost, but as a vibrant celebration of who she had been. A garden. A memorial garden. The words themselves held a quiet promise, a soft melody against the harsh cacophony of their grief.

She approached Shawn with a trepidation that belied the growing conviction in her heart. Her voice, when she finally spoke, was soft, almost hesitant, as if afraid to disturb the fragile peace that had settled over him, or perhaps, more accurately, over his silence. "Shawn," she began, her gaze fixed on the swirling patterns in his coffee, "I've been thinking."

He stirred slightly, a subtle shift of his weight, but his eyes remained fixed on some point beyond the chipped ceramic mug. His silence, once a source of sharp pain, had become a habitual response, a learned defense mechanism. Yet, Kate persisted, her voice gaining a fragile strength.

"About Mae," she continued, the name, a gentle caress in the quiet room. "About... about remembering her. Properly." She paused, searching for the right words, for a way to articulate a vision that felt so clear to her, yet so vulnerable to misinterpretation. "I was thinking... What if we created something for her? Something... living."

He finally looked at her then, his eyes, usually clouded with a weariness that seemed to seep from his very bones, holding a flicker of... what? Curiosity? Confusion? Or perhaps just the dull reflex of acknowledgement. His brow furrowed, a faint question etched into his features.

Kate took a deep breath, a physical act of gathering courage. "A garden," she said, the word clearer now, imbued with the tentative hope that propelled it. "For Mae. A place... a place where we can go, where we can remember her. Where we can plant things she would have loved." She pictured it then, vividly: a riot of color, the sweet scent of flowers, the buzz of bees, a sanctuary from the sterile, suffocating reality of their apartment. "We could put in those bright yellow sunflowers she adored," she mused aloud, a faint smile touching her lips, "and maybe some lavender, like the kind that grew by her grandmother's house. And perhaps a small bench, where we could sit... together."

The emphasis on "together" was almost involuntary, a desperate plea woven into the fabric of her suggestion. She knew, with a crushing certainty, that this wasn't just about creating a memorial; it was about finding a way back to each other, a shared project that could serve as a lifeline in the turbulent waters of their shared grief. This wasn't a demand, or an accusation, or even a plea for him to acknowledge her pain directly. It was an offering, a gentle proposition, a tentative hand extended across the desolate landscape of their fractured marriage.

Shawn's gaze remained steady for a moment, his expression unreadable. The silence stretched, taut and expectant. Kate braced herself for the familiar wall of indifference, the dismissive shrug, the muttered word that would signal the death of her fragile hope. But then, slowly, almost imperceptibly, a subtle change occurred. The tightness around his jaw seemed to soften, the hard lines of his face easing. He didn't speak, not immediately, but his eyes, those windows to a soul she felt she had lost touch with, held a flicker of something that wasn't outright rejection. It was a hesitant engagement, a fragile opening, the smallest of cracks in the armor he had so carefully constructed around himself.

"A garden?" he finally echoed, his voice a low murmur, devoid of its usual gruffness. It wasn't an enthusiastic agreement, not by any stretch of the imagination, but it wasn't a dismissal either. It was a question, an inquiry, a sign that her words, her carefully chosen words, had managed to penetrate the fog that had enveloped him.

Kate's heart gave a little leap, a tentative flutter of hope. "Yes," she affirmed, her voice gaining a little more confidence. "A garden. For Mae. We could... We could start small. Maybe find a patch of ground somewhere. Or even... even just pots on the balcony, if that's easier to start with." She was willing to compromise, to scale down her grand vision if it meant finding a foothold, a shared activity that could begin to mend the frayed edges of their lives. "It would be a place to... to keep her memory alive. To show her we haven't forgotten."

She watched him closely, her breath held, dissecting every nuance of his reaction. The idea of a garden, a place of growth and life, felt like a stark contrast to the stagnation that had taken hold of their lives. It was an act of faith, a belief that beauty could still emerge from sorrow, that healing could begin with a simple act of creation. She wasn't sure if Shawn's grief was as all-consuming as hers, or if it manifested in a different, more internalized way, but she knew that something needed to be done, something proactive, something that didn't involve the endless rehashing of pain or the suffocating embrace of silence.

Shawn didn't laugh with her, but he didn't flinch away either. He remained still, his expression thoughtful, as if he were turning her words over in his mind, sifting through the layers of their shared past. It was in these quiet moments, these brief interludes of shared memory, that Kate saw glimmers of the man she had loved, the man who had once been her anchor, her confidant, her greatest joy.

"We could... we could visit a nursery," Kate ventured, pushing the boundaries of her comfort zone. "Just to look. See what's available. No pressure. Just... see." She held her breath, waiting for his response. This was the crucial moment. The proposition, so delicate and tentative, hung in the balance. Would he retreat, or would he take another small step forward?

"Maybe," he said, his voice still quiet, but carrying a new inflection. It was a word pregnant with possibility, a whisper of consent. "Maybe. We could... look."

Kate's breath hitched. It wasn't a resounding yes, not a declaration of renewed purpose, but it was more than she had dared to hope for. It was an opening. A sliver of light breaking through the perpetual twilight of their lives. It was the first tentative step towards a shared endeavor, a common ground where their individual griefs might, just might, begin to find a shared space for healing. She felt a surge of gratitude, so potent it threatened to bring tears to her eyes, tears not of sorrow, but of a fragile, burgeoning hope. This gentle proposition, born from a place of profound love and a desperate yearning for remembrance, had landed, not with a bang, but with a soft, hopeful whisper. It was a seed, planted in the barren soil of their despair, and for the first time in a long time, Kate dared to believe it might actually grow.

Chapter 13

The scent of lavender and the bright, defiant faces of sunflowers had, for a time, been enough. They had been beacons in the encroaching fog, tangible proofs that life, however battered, could still find a way to bloom. Kate's quiet strength, her unwavering presence beside him as they'd worked the soil, had been an anchor. It wasn't a spoken forgiveness, not an erasure of the hurts, but a silent testament to a shared grief that was slowly, painstakingly, becoming a shared path forward. Yet, beneath the veneer of burgeoning hope, the old demons stirred, their whispers growing louder, more insistent. The alcohol, once a clumsy anesthetic, had become a thief, not just of his senses, but of his very will.

He'd started noticing the patterns, the insidious creep of dependency. It wasn't just the solitary drinking anymore; it was the pre-emptive swallow before facing Kate, the hurried gulp to numb the sharp edges of memory, the desperate need to blur the stark reality of his grief into something more manageable. But it was a false management, a surrender disguised as coping. Each drink was a betrayal, a step further away from the man he wanted to be, the man Mae deserved, the man Kate needed. The garden, the quiet ritual of tending to it, had offered a sanctuary, a space where the suffocating weight of his loss felt a little lighter. He could lose himself in the rhythm of watering, the feel of the earth crumbling between his fingers, the simple, undeniable act of nurturing life. But when the sun dipped below the horizon, and the quiet descended, the thirst would return, a gnawing emptiness that only the burn of liquor seemed to fill.

The realization had hit him like a physical blow one evening, not in the quiet of his grief, but in the hollow echo of his own self-deception. He'd been sitting on the balcony, watching Kate tend to the roses, her silhouette etched against the twilight sky. She was a picture of quiet resilience, her movements deliberate, her focus unwavering. He'd reached for his usual nightly solace, the familiar weight of the bottle in his hand, when a wave of nausea washed over him. It wasn't the alcohol itself, but the act. The sheer, abject shame of it. He saw himself, not as a grieving husband, a devoted father trying to honour his daughter's memory, but as a man drowning, his own hands pulling him under. The garden was a vibrant testament to life, to growth, to a future. His drinking was a testament to his refusal to participate in any of it.

The image of Mae, not as a ghost in his memory, but as a vibrant presence, flashed behind his eyes. What would she think of him? This man, slurring his words, his hands trembling, seeking oblivion in a bottle? The thought was a cold, sharp shard of ice in his gut. He wanted to be worthy of her memory, not a cautionary tale of a life unlived, of potential squandered.

He looked at Kate, her brow furrowed in concentration as she gently pruned a stray branch. She had borne so much, endured so much, and yet, here she was, creating beauty from ashes, her love for Mae a constant, unwavering force. And he had been... what? Hiding? Flinching? Drowning his sorrows while she bravely faced the tide? The contrast was stark, a brutal mirror held up to his own cowardice. He felt a desperate need to connect, to bridge the chasm that his addiction had created between them, but the words wouldn't come. He could only feel the familiar tightening in his chest, the urge to reach for the bottle to ease the burgeoning panic.

The memory garden, a project born of shared pain, had become an unintended catalyst for his awakening. Each plant, each bloom, was a deliberate act of remembrance, a step towards healing. He saw it in Kate's eyes, in the subtle softening of her features as she spoke of Mae's favorite flowers. He saw it in himself, in the fleeting moments of peace he found while working the earth. But the peace was fragile, easily shattered by the insistent craving. He understood, with a clarity that was both terrifying and exhilarating, that he couldn't tend to the garden, couldn't truly honour Mae, couldn't possibly rebuild his life, if he continued to be enslaved by the bottle.

He put the bottle down, the clink of glass on the terracotta pot a surprisingly loud sound in the quiet evening. His hand trembled, not from the need for a drink, but from the sheer effort of resistance. It was a small gesture, almost imperceptible, but it felt like a monumental shift. He watched Kate, her head tilted, listening, as if sensing the change in the air, the subtle shift in his energy. She didn't speak, didn't demand, didn't pry. Her presence was a quiet affirmation, a testament to the enduring strength of their bond, a bond he had been systematically eroding.

The internal battle raged. The ingrained habits, the psychological crutches, screamed for release. The voice of addiction was a siren song, promising oblivion, promising relief from the gnawing emptiness. But another voice was emerging, stronger, clearer – the voice of his own will, amplified by the love for his daughter and the quiet strength of his wife. It was the voice that whispered of a life beyond the haze, a life of clarity, of purpose, of genuine connection. It was the voice that reminded him of the man he was before the darkness descended, the man who had promised Mae the world, the man who had promised Kate forever.

He closed his eyes, picturing Mae's face, her smile, her bright, unblemished spirit. He saw her running through a sun-drenched field, her laughter echoing on the wind. Shawn constantly imagined the life he would have lived with his daughter.

He opened his eyes, his gaze finding Kate. The words, when they finally came, were raw, unpracticed, and deeply imperfect. "Kate," he began, his voice rough, unaccustomed to such honesty. He paused, searching for the right words, the words that could convey the depth of his realization, the magnitude of his struggle. The silence stretched, pregnant with unspoken emotions. He could feel her waiting, her gaze steady, a silent question in her eyes. This was it. The precipice. The moment of decision. The choice between succumbing to the darkness or stepping, however tentatively, towards the light. The memory garden, with its vibrant colours and living promise, had shown him what was possible. Now, he had to find the courage to fight for it, to fight for himself, for them, for Mae. He took a deep, shuddering breath, the air filling his lungs, a tangible sign of life, of possibility. He was ready to fight. He had to be.

Chapter 14

The stillness of the night was a deceptive calm. Outside, the crickets chirped their relentless song, a familiar soundtrack to the hushed landscape of his grief. Inside, however, a storm was brewing. The decision, once made, felt less like a victory and more like the surrender of a besieged city. The bottle, that once-trusted companion, now sat on the sideboard, a dark sentinel, its presence a constant, taunting reminder of the escape it offered. Shawn's hand hovered near it, an involuntary twitch, a phantom limb reaching for a phantom solace. This was the precipice, the edge of the abyss, and he had willingly stepped to the brink.

The first twenty-four hours were a brutal, relentless war waged within the confines of his own body and mind. Sleep was a distant memory, chased away by a restless anxiety that clawed at his insides. His head throbbed with a dull, persistent ache, a physical manifestation of the internal turmoil. Every nerve ending seemed to hum with an amplified sensitivity, the softest sounds grating, the slightest touch sending tremors through him. It was as if his system, deprived of its accustomed poison, was screaming in protest, demanding its due. His thoughts, usually a chaotic but familiar jumble, now raced with a terrifying clarity, each memory, each regret, each fear amplified tenfold. The faces of the past, Mae's bright smile, her innocent questions, her sudden absence, all loomed large, unbidden and overwhelming. Without the numbing haze of alcohol, the raw, unvarnished pain of her loss was a constant, searing presence.

Kate, bless her quiet strength, was a silent pillar of support. She moved through the house with a gentle grace, her presence a comforting balm without the need for words. She made tea, her fingers brushing Shawn's as she handed me the warm mug, a simple gesture that spoke volumes. She would sit with him, sometimes in companionable silence, other times with a soft question about his day, a gentle inquiry that didn't pry but simply offered an opening. He saw the worry etched around her eyes, the subtle tension in her shoulders, and the guilt gnawed at me. He was adding to her burden, a burden she already carried with such stoic resilience. His addiction had been a secret thief, stealing not just his peace, but a measure of hers too. Now, in his attempt to reclaim himself, he was acutely aware of the collateral damage, the love and support he had taken for granted, the emotional toll his self-destruction had inflicted.

The physical withdrawal was a humbling, terrifying ordeal. Shawn's hands trembled uncontrollably, a constant tremor that made simple tasks, like holding a glass or turning a page, a Herculean effort. His stomach churned, a nauseous tide that ebbed and flowed, leaving him weak and depleted. Hot flashes would sweep over him without warning, drenching his skin in a clammy sweat, followed by shivers that rattled his bones. It felt like his body was staging a violent rebellion, a desperate attempt to purge itself of the foreign invader he had so readily invited in. Each ache, each tremor, each wave of nausea was a stark reminder of the physical grip alcohol had on him, a grip he had been too blind, too afraid, or too consumed by grief to acknowledge.

Beyond the physical torment, the psychological battle was even more insidious. The cravings were like a physical hunger, a gnawing emptiness that demanded to be filled. They would arise out of nowhere, triggered by the most innocuous things – the sight of a half-empty bottle in the recycling bin, the distant clink of glasses from a neighbor's party, even the subtle scent of something reminiscent of a bar. These cravings weren't just a fleeting desire; they were a desperate, primal urge, a siren song promising instant relief, a temporary oblivion from the suffocating weight of his own thoughts and emotions. The voice of addiction whispered seductive lies, telling me Shawn that he deserved a break, that just one drink wouldn't hurt, that this suffering was too much to bear. It preyed on his weakness, on his grief, on his profound sense of loneliness.

It was in those moments of near-surrender that the memory of Mae's face would flicker, a beacon in the encroaching darkness. Shawn would see her, not as a victim of his negligence, but as a vibrant, inquisitive child, full of life and wonder. What would she think of me now, this man consumed by despair and self-pity? The thought of her disappointment, of her confusion, was a potent antidote to the craving. She deserved better. She deserved a father who was present, who was strong, who could carry her memory with dignity and grace, not with the shame of addiction.

Kate found Shawn like that, his forehead pressed against the cool glass of the windowpane, tears silently streaming down his face. She didn't say anything at first. She simply came and stood beside him, her hand gently resting on his back. Her touch was a silent anchor, a tangible reassurance that he wasn't entirely alone in this tempest.

"It's hard," she whispered, her voice barely audible. "But you're doing it. You're really doing it." Her words, simple and true, cut through the fog of his despair. They were not platitudes, but observations, acknowledgments of the immense effort he was making.

Her unwavering belief, even when his own was faltering, became a vital source of strength. It was a quiet force, an unspoken contract of mutual support that had been forged in the crucible of our shared loss. Shawn realized then that while his grief was a solitary burden, his recovery didn't have to be. Kate's presence was a constant reminder of the life they still had, the future they could still build, however fragile it might seem.

The garden, once a sanctuary, now became a battleground for Shawn's resolve. The act of tending to the plants, the grounding rhythm of digging, planting, and watering, became a form of active meditation. It was a way to channel the restless energy, to focus his scattered thoughts. When the cravings hit, he would force himself outside, the fresh air and the scent of damp earth a welcome distraction. He would pull weeds with an almost ferocious intensity, each uprooted weed a symbolic victory over the destructive tendencies within me. The sunflowers, their faces turned towards the sun, seemed to mock his despair with their unwavering optimism. Their silent resilience was a lesson, a reminder that even after the harshest winter, life could, and would, bloom again.

There were days when the struggle felt insurmountable. Days when the physical symptoms were so debilitating that Shawn could barely function. Days when the emotional pain was so raw that he felt like he was being torn apart. On those days, the thought of surrendering, of drowning the agony in a bottle, was a constant, gnawing temptation. It was a testament to the insidious nature of addiction, how it could twist even the most profound love into a justification for self-destruction.

The path to sobriety was not a straight line, but a winding, often treacherous road. There were stumbles, relapses, moments when the grip of addiction threatened to pull him back into its dark embrace. But each time, he found himself drawn back to the anchors of his support system – Kate's steady love, the quiet solace of the garden, the understanding faces at the support group. These were the lights that guided him through the darkness, the reminders that even in his weakest moments, he was not beyond redemption.

Shawn's physical symptoms gradually subsided, replaced by a different kind of ache – the ache of confronting his emotions, of processing his grief without the artificial balm of alcohol. The mental fog began to lift, revealing a clarity that was both exhilarating and daunting. He started to feel again, truly feel, the sharp edges of his sadness, the lingering tendrils of guilt, but also the burgeoning shoots of hope, the rediscovery of joy in the simple things.

One evening, Shawn found himself sitting on the porch swing, watching the sunset paint the sky in hues of orange and purple. Kate's favorite flowers, the daisies, stood tall and proud in the garden, their faces turned towards the fading light. For the first time in a long time, he felt a sense of peace, a quiet contentment that wasn't dependent on the numbing effect of alcohol. The cravings were still there, a faint whisper in the background, but they no longer held the same power. They were shadows, not the substance of his reality.

Kate joined Shawn, settling beside him on the swing, her hand finding his. They sat in comfortable silence, watching the sky fade to twilight. The air was cool and still, carrying the faint scent of jasmine from the garden. He looked at her, at the lines of worry that were slowly softening around her eyes, and felt a surge of gratitude so profound it brought tears to his eyes. "Thank you," he whispered, the words catching in his throat.

She squeezed his hand. "We're doing this together," she replied, her voice soft but firm. And in that moment, he knew she was right. Sobriety was not just his battle; it was a testament to the enduring strength of their bond, a bond that had weathered the storm and was slowly, painstakingly, finding its way back to the light.

The first steps were the hardest, a testament to the sheer, unadulterated will it took to reclaim oneself from the clutches of addiction. But with each hesitant step, with each small victory, the path ahead, though still challenging, began to feel navigable, illuminated by the quiet strength of love and the unwavering promise of a new dawn.

Chapter 15

The silence between Kate and Shawn had become a landscape of its own, a vast, unexplored territory born from years of unspoken truths and broken promises. Now, in the fragile dawn of his sobriety, this silence felt different. It wasn't the heavy, suffocating quiet of avoidance, but a hesitant pause, pregnant with the possibility of rediscovery. The bottle, that gluttonous thief of honesty, was gone. Yet, its shadow lingered, a specter of doubt that haunted Kate's eyes whenever she looked at him. Rebuilding trust wasn't about grand gestures or eloquent apologies; it was a granular, painstaking process, woven from the threads of everyday interactions. It was about showing up, consistently, unequivocally, as the man he claimed to be.

His first step, and perhaps the most terrifying, was to shed the armor of his internal monologue. For so long, he had operated in a world of rationalizations, where his drinking was a consequence of external pressures, a balm for his grief, anything but a personal failing. Now, the demand was for radical honesty, not just with Kate, but with himself. Shawn began to articulate the swirling chaos within him, even when it felt raw and shameful. The cravings that gnawed at his resolve, the fear that gripped him when he faced a particularly difficult memory, the sheer exhaustion of maintaining sobriety – these were no longer whispered secrets, but spoken words.

"I had a strong urge today, Kate," Shawn would say, his voice catching with the effort of admitting his weakness. "Saw a group of guys at the pub, laughing, and for a moment, I just wanted to be back there, to forget."

These confessions were met not with immediate absolution, but with a quiet, discerning gaze. She listened, her expression unreadable, her silence a space for me to continue, to unpack the layers of his vulnerability. It was a far cry from the easy acceptance he had once taken for granted. Her cautious observation was a constant reminder of the chasm he had created, a chasm he had to bridge, one honest word at a time.

This wasn't just about verbalizing his struggles; it was about demonstrating a fundamental shift in his behavior. The late nights spent in a haze were replaced by early mornings, where Shawn would be up before Kate, making coffee, tidying the kitchen, a quiet prelude to the day ahead. The neglected responsibilities that had piled up during his drinking years began to be addressed. It was the mundane, the domestic, the ordinary that became the bedrock of his newfound integrity. He started fixing the leaky faucet that had been dripping for months, a small act of repair that felt disproportionately significant. He tackled the overgrown garden, not with the manic intensity of his early sobriety, but with a steady, sustained effort, the physical labor a tangible manifestation of his commitment to growth and order.

Kate observed these changes with a quiet intensity. She didn't offer effusive praise, a reflex that might have felt hollow given the history of Shawn's grand pronouncements and subsequent failures. Instead, her acknowledgment was subtle, often found in the softening of her posture, a faint smile that touched the corners of her lips, or the way she would meet his gaze with a flicker of something that resembled hope. One evening, after he had spent hours meticulously repairing a wobbly fence post that had been an eyesore for years, she simply said, "You did a good job with that, Shawn." The understated nature of her compliment was more potent than any gushing affirmation could have been. It was a recognition of sustained effort, of tangible progress, not just a fleeting moment of good behavior.

The intimacy they had lost, suffocated by his addiction and the secrets it spawned, was another casualty he desperately needed to reclaim. The physical touch that had once been a natural expression of their connection had become fraught with a new kind of tension. His fear of relapse, coupled with his awareness of her lingering doubt, created a hesitance in Shawn, a self-consciousness that was alien to their former selves. He longed to reach for Kate, to hold her close, but the thought of appearing desperate, or worse, of triggering a sense of unease in her, held him back.

It was Kate who, in her own quiet way, began to bridge this gap. One evening, as they sat on the sofa, the television a low murmur in the background, she reached out and laid her hand on Shawn's knee. It was a simple gesture, devoid of expectation, yet it resonated with a profound significance. He didn't recoil, didn't pull away. Instead, he tentatively placed his hand over hers, their fingers intertwining. Her grip was firm, steady. It wasn't a passionate embrace, but it was a connection, a silent acknowledgment that they were still here, still capable of finding solace in each other's presence.

"I'm still scared, you know," she admitted one night, her voice barely a whisper. They were in bed, the darkness a familiar confessional. "Every time you're late, or when you seem quiet, a part of me still tenses up." Her honesty was a gift, a raw, unvarnished truth that he desperately needed to hear. It allowed him to understand the depth of the emotional scar tissue he had created. It wasn't just about his actions; it was about the indelible imprint they had left on her.

"I know," Shawn replied, his voice thick with emotion. "And I don't blame you for it. All I can do is keep showing you that I'm here, that I'm not going back. You deserve to feel safe, Kate. And I'm going to do everything I can to make sure you do." His words felt inadequate, a pale imitation of the immense reassurance he wanted to convey. But they were honest, and they were accompanied by a renewed determination to back them up with consistent action.

The process of rebuilding trust wasn't linear. There were days when a flicker of the old doubt would cross Kate's face, a fleeting shadow that would send a jolt of anxiety through him. A stressful day at work, a minor disagreement, even a seemingly innocuous comment could trigger a moment of uncertainty. In those instances, his instinct was to retreat, to become defensive, to withdraw into the familiar shell of self-protection. But he was learning to fight that instinct. Instead of withdrawing, Shawn learned to lean in, to address the unspoken anxiety directly.

Their communication, once a battlefield of accusations and defensiveness, began to transform into a dialogue of mutual understanding. They started having regular "check-ins," not formal, stilted affairs, but informal conversations where they could share their thoughts and feelings about their recovery, their relationship, and their individual well-being. These weren't always easy conversations. There were moments of frustration, of tears, of raw emotional vulnerability. But each time they navigated these difficult waters together, their bond grew stronger, their trust more resilient.

Shawn learned to anticipate Kate's needs, not through telepathy, but through attentive observation. He noticed the subtle signs of stress on her face after a particularly demanding day, and he would try to lighten her load, whether by taking on more household chores, offering a listening ear, or simply creating a quiet, comforting atmosphere. He remembered the things she loved – her favorite tea, the books she wanted to read, the quiet evenings spent in conversation – and he made an effort to incorporate them back into their lives. These weren't grand romantic gestures, but small, consistent acts of thoughtfulness that spoke volumes about his renewed commitment to their marriage.

There were times when he felt an almost overwhelming sense of guilt for the pain he had inflicted. The memories of Kate's tear-streaked face, her quiet despair, the countless times Shawn had let her down, would surface with a sharp, visceral pang. In those moments, he would remind myself that dwelling on the past was a form of self-indulgence that wouldn't serve either of them. Instead, he focused on the present, on the tangible steps he was taking to build a better future. His energy was directed towards creating new memories, positive ones, that would gradually overwrite the painful ones.

The rebuilding of their intimacy was a slow, deliberate process. It wasn't a return to the way things were, but a cautious exploration of a new landscape. They learned to communicate their desires, their boundaries, their vulnerabilities in a way they never had before. The tentative touches, the shared glances, the quiet evenings spent in each other's company – these became the building blocks of a renewed connection, one that was more profound, more honest, and ultimately, more resilient.

One evening, months into Shawn's sobriety, they were sitting on the porch swing, watching the fireflies dance in the twilight. The air was warm and humid, carrying the scent of blooming jasmine. Kate leaned her head on his shoulder, a gesture that was no longer tentative, but natural, comfortable. He wrapped his arm around her, pulling her closer.

"You know," she murmured, her voice soft, "there are still times when a little piece of me holds its breath. When I see you stressed, or when you're quiet for too long."

Shawn held her tighter. "I know. And I understand. I'm not asking you to forget. I'm just asking you to believe in what we're building together."

She turned her head, her eyes meeting his in the dim light. There was a vulnerability in her gaze, but also a strength, a newfound resolve. "I am," she said, her voice firm. "I believe in what we're building. It's... different now. Stronger, maybe. Because we're both putting in the work."

Chapter 16

The bravest thing Shawn learned to do wasn't to face down the physical cravings, nor to intellectualize the psychological demons. It was to admit, out loud, with no embellishment or excuse, that he was lost. That he was hurting. That he didn't have all the answers, and that the path ahead felt impossibly steep. For so long, his identity had been intertwined with a stoic self-sufficiency, a quiet competence that masked a deep-seated fear of appearing weak. To confess a moment of doubt, a tremor of fear, felt like an admission of fundamental failure. Alcohol had been his foolproof shield, a way to project an image of control even when he was unraveling from the inside. But in sobriety, that shield was gone, leaving me exposed, raw, and surprisingly, far more capable of genuine connection.

This newfound willingness to be vulnerable wasn't a sudden epiphany; it was a slow, arduous process, like coaxing a shy animal out of its burrow. It began in those quiet moments with Kate, where the usual pretense of normalcy fell away. Instead of recounting his day with a practiced air of stoicism, he started sharing the small anxieties, the lingering sadness, the moments where the memory of Mae or the echo of his father's quiet disapproval would pierce through his resolve.

"I had a tough time today, Kate," He'd say, the admission itself a victory. "I almost picked up a drink this afternoon. The urge was... intense." There was no longer shame in these confessions, only a quiet honesty that, in turn, invited her own. She would reach for Shawn's hand, her touch a silent affirmation, and share her own struggles, her own moments of feeling overwhelmed.

This sharing wasn't about seeking pity or validation, though a measure of both often followed. It was about the act of externalizing the internal chaos, of letting it breathe in the open air rather than festering in the dark confines of his own mind. It was about recognizing that the strength Shawn had so desperately sought in isolation was, in fact, amplified by sharing his burdens. His therapist, Dr. Evans, had been instrumental in this shift. He'd gently steered me away from the narrative of being a victim and towards the empowering reality of agency. "Shawn," he'd said, his voice calm and steady, "your power doesn't come from never feeling pain. It comes from how you choose to respond to it. And choosing to reach out, to admit you're struggling, that's one of the most powerful responses there is."

Shawn started to see vulnerability not as a weakness, but as a courageous act of self-acceptance. It was the conscious decision to let down his guard, to allow others to see the imperfections, the rough edges, the parts of myself that he had spent years hiding. This meant being honest not just with Kate, but with myself. It meant acknowledging the fear that lay beneath his anger, the insecurity that fueled his defensiveness, the profound sadness that alcohol had so effectively anesthetized.

The profound impact of this vulnerability was most evident in Shawn's relationship with Kate. The wall of silence and unspoken resentments that had separated us for so long began to crumble. By admitting his own failings, his own struggles with grief and addiction, he created space for her to share her own. She spoke of the loneliness she felt, the fear that had gripped her as she watched me descend into alcoholism, the silent burden she carried of holding our family together. Her honesty was a revelation, a mirror reflecting the years of her own unspoken pain.

"I felt so invisible, Shawn," she confessed one evening, her voice soft with years of held-back emotion. "When you were drinking, it was like you were in another world, and I was just on the outside, watching. I missed you. I missed *us*. And I didn't know how to reach you." Her words were a poignant testament to the collateral damage of his addiction, a reminder that his self-destructive behavior had cast a long shadow over the people he loved most.

Their shared vulnerability became a bridge, allowing them to navigate the wreckage of their past and begin the painstaking work of rebuilding. They started to talk about Mae, not just as a painful memory, but as a shared connection, a love that had shaped them both. They sifted through old photographs, recalling stories, laughing at her quirks, and yes, sometimes weeping for her absence. These moments, infused with honesty and shared emotion, were more healing than any attempt to simply "get over" the grief. They were about integrating the loss into the fabric of their lives, acknowledging that the pain of her absence was intertwined with the enduring power of her love.

This journey into vulnerability wasn't a destination, but a continuous practice. There were still days when the urge to retreat into his own head, to armor himself against the world, was strong for Shawn. The fear of judgment, the ingrained habit of self-reliance, would sometimes resurface. But now, he has a counter-narrative. He had the memory of how opening up had led to connection, how admitting weakness had paradoxically made him stronger, how letting others see his struggles had, in fact, fostered deeper love and understanding.

Shawn learned to recognize the subtle shifts in his own emotional landscape, the early warning signs of withdrawal or self-deception. Instead of suppressing these feelings, he would acknowledge them. "I'm feeling a bit lost today," he might say to Kate. Or, "I'm feeling overwhelmed by the past, and I'm struggling to stay present." These simple affirmations, spoken aloud, seemed to dissipate their power. They were no longer lurking threats, but acknowledged challenges that could be met with intention and support.

This transformation was a quiet revolution within him. It was the dismantling of a fortress built on denial and self-protection, and the slow, deliberate construction of a sanctuary built on honesty and connection. The strength Shawn found wasn't in the absence of pain or fear, but in the courage to confront them, to admit his limitations, and to lean into the support of those who loved him. It was a testament to the profound truth that sometimes, the most powerful way to heal is to be truly seen, in all our imperfect, vulnerable humanity. The demons of his past hadn't vanished, but they no longer held absolute dominion. They were now a part of his story, acknowledged and understood, but no longer dictating the narrative. And in that acknowledgment, in that willingness to be truly open, lay a resilient, enduring strength that he had never known he possessed. His vulnerability was no longer a liability; it was his greatest asset, the very foundation of his renewed life.

Chapter 17

As the sun rose on Shawn's 26th birthday, he couldn't help but sit down and reflect on the events of the last 12 months. He sat here, having just celebrated a 3rd wedding anniversary with a woman who he had to overcome immeasurable tragedy within just one long year.

26 was supposed to just be the other side of your twenties. Shawn knew he was supposed to be planning the first birthday of his first child. This was supposed to just be a moment on his way to bigger and more momentous occasions in his and Kate's life.

A year closer to... what? A year further from her. It was a marker he'd been dreading, an arbitrary point in time that felt loaded with the weight of his own perceived failures, his inability to conjure the effervescent joy that birthdays had once represented. The thought of celebrating, of marking a year without her, had seemed almost grotesque, a cruel mockery of the life she had been so brutally robbed of.

But the apprehension that had once coiled in his stomach had, with a surprising gentleness, begun to unspool. It hadn't vanished entirely, of course. Grief, he was learning, was not a monolith to be conquered and discarded. It was more like the tide, an ebb and flow, its presence felt even in its retreat. Yet, on this particular morning, the tide felt low, leaving behind a shore of quiet contentment.

Kate had insisted on a small gathering. Not a party, she'd stressed, her hand finding Shawn's across the breakfast table, her eyes holding a plea for understanding. "Just... a few of us," she'd murmured, her voice still a little raspy from sleep. "A quiet lunch. Here. In the garden room. In Mae's room."

And so, here they were. The garden room, bathed in the soft light of early afternoon, was filled with the quiet murmur of a few cherished voices. A few family and friends stopped in to enjoy the peace. Liam, Shawn's oldest friend, his presence a steady anchor, sat in a wicker chair, nursing a cup of tea, his usual easy grin in place. And Sarah, Liam's partner, her warmth a soothing balm, was showing Kate a collection of photographs she'd found from a camping trip years ago, the laughter that rippled through the room a sound that no longer felt jarring, but rather, like a welcome melody.

There was no grand cake, no forced revelry. Instead, a simple table was laid with a checkered cloth, laden with a selection of their favorite foods. It was understated, intimate, and deeply resonant. It was a celebration of life, not a denial of loss, and for the first time in a long time, that felt not just permissible, but profoundly right.

But the world, in its quiet, persistent way, had found its way in. It had seeped through the cracks, through the tentative conversations with Kate, through the shared silences that had gradually become less heavy, through the rediscovery of the garden, through the simple act of taking a deep breath of fresh air. It had started with small gestures, almost imperceptible shifts in perspective. The robin in the autumn garden, the humming in the quiet evening, the act of pruning the overgrown roses – each had been a tiny seed of resilience planted in the barren soil of his sorrow.

This birthday, then, was not a jarring departure from the past, but a natural evolution. It was the culmination of countless small victories, of quiet moments of courage. It was proof that the profound loss Shawn had endured had not broken him entirely, but had, in fact, reshaped him. The scars were there, deep and undeniable, but they were no longer gaping wounds. They were becoming part of the landscape, reminders of a journey that had been brutally difficult, but ultimately, one that had led him back towards the light.

He caught Kate's eye across the table. She offered Shawn a smile, a soft, knowing smile that spoke volumes without a single word. It was a smile that acknowledged the darkness they had navigated, the depths of despair they had plumbed, and the quiet strength they had found in each other, and within themselves, to emerge into this new dawn. It was a smile of shared understanding, of enduring love, and of a hope that was no longer a fragile whisper, but a steady, unwavering flame.

Chapter 18

The world, once a place of stark contrasts, of blinding light and crushing darkness, had gradually softened, its edges blurring into a more nuanced spectrum. It wasn't that the pain had vanished entirely, or that the ache had miraculously healed into a scar that was no longer felt. Rather, it had settled, a quiet undercurrent beneath the surface of everyday life, a constant reminder of the depths Shawn and Kate had plumbed. But within this settled state, a new form of existence had begun to bloom. They were learning, painstakingly at first, then with a growing, almost defiant rhythm, to build a life that was not just *after* the loss, but *with* it.

This wasn't a resurrection of the past, a desperate attempt to recreate the effervescent joy that had once defined their days. That was an impossible task, and one they had long since abandoned. Instead, it was a conscious, deliberate act of weaving the threads of their present into the fabric of their history, acknowledging the intricate patterns of love, loss, and the enduring strength that had emerged from the crucible of their suffering. It was about finding the small, quiet pockets of beauty that had always existed, but which they had been too preoccupied, too blinded by the magnitude of their sorrow, to truly see.

For Shawn and Kate, this meant rediscovering the simple pleasures that had once been the bedrock of their shared life. A quiet morning, the aroma of coffee brewing, the gentle murmur of conversation as they planned their day – these were no longer taken for granted. Each moment, stripped of its former predictability, now carried a weight of its own, a fragile preciousness that demanded their full attention. They learned to savor the taste of a meal, the warmth of the sun on their skin, the comfortable silence that could exist between them without the need for forced cheerfulness. These were not grand gestures, but subtle shifts in perception, a recalibration of their senses to the enduring miracles of ordinary life.

The question of "purpose" had loomed large in the aftermath. What was the point of continuing, of striving, when the very core of their family had been so brutally fractured? For a long time, there was no answer, only a dull, persistent emptiness. But as the sharp edges of grief began to wear down, a new understanding began to dawn. Their purpose wasn't a singular, grand design waiting to be discovered, but rather a mosaic, pieced together from countless small acts of intention. It was in the way they nurtured their relationships, the quiet support they offered each other, the conscious effort to extend kindness and understanding to those around them.

Kate found herself drawn back to her writing, not with the same frantic urgency as before, but with a deeper, more reflective spirit. The words, once a refuge from pain, now became a conduit for understanding. She began to write not just about the sorrow, but about the resilience, about the unexpected beauty that could be found even in the ruins. She explored the ways in which loss had reshaped their perspectives, forcing them to confront their own mortality and, in doing so, to cherish life with a newfound intensity. Her stories became a testament to the human capacity to endure, to adapt, and ultimately, to find meaning even in the face of unimaginable heartbreak.

Shawn, in his own way, embarked on a similar journey of rediscovery. He had always been a man of quiet action, and his work, though demanding, had always provided him with a sense of structure. But now, he infused it with a different kind of passion. He spoke of the importance of mentorship, of guiding the younger generation with the wisdom he had gleaned from his own experiences. He began volunteering at a local community center, sharing his skills and offering a steady presence to those who were struggling. It wasn't about seeking recognition or validation, but about the inherent satisfaction of contributing, of making a tangible difference in the lives of others.

Shawn and Kate's social interactions also underwent a transformation. The superficialities of past acquaintances began to fall away, replaced by a deeper appreciation for genuine connection. They sought out friendships that were built on honesty, on vulnerability, and on a shared understanding of life's complexities. They learned to be more present in their conversations, to listen with greater empathy, and to offer support without judgment. They discovered that true community wasn't about endless social engagements, but about the quiet comfort of knowing you were not alone, that there were others who understood the delicate dance between joy and sorrow.

There were still moments, of course, when the weight of their loss would descend with a familiar heaviness. A particular song on the radio, a child's laughter, a scent carried on the breeze – these could, without warning, stir the deep waters of their grief. In those instances, Shawn and Kate no longer fought against the emotions. Instead, they acknowledged them, allowed themselves to feel the sting, and then, with a quiet strength, they would find their way back to the present. It was a conscious choice, a reaffirmation of their commitment to living fully, to embracing the entirety of their experience, the good and the painful, as integral parts of who they had become.

One of the most profound lessons they learned was the power of forgiveness, not just for others, but for themselves. They had carried a burden of guilt, of "what ifs" and "if onlys," for so long. Had we done enough? Could we have prevented it? These questions, while often unvoiced, had been a constant companion. Through countless conversations, through shared tears and quiet introspection, they began to release themselves from these self-imposed shackles. They understood that they had loved Mae with every fiber of their being, and that was enough. Perfection was an illusion, and true strength lay in accepting our humanity, our limitations, and our unwavering love.

The concept of "moving on" had always felt like a betrayal, a suggestion that they should leave Mae behind, as if her memory were a burden to be shed. But as they moved forward, they realized that it wasn't about moving on, but about moving *with* her. Her spirit, her love – these had become an intrinsic part of them. They informed their decisions, guided their actions, and enriched their lives in ways they could never have anticipated. Her legacy wasn't one of sorrow, but one of enduring love, a testament to the profound impact one small life could have on the tapestry of existence.

Shawn and Kate's home, once a shrine to their grief, had slowly transformed into a sanctuary of remembrance and a vibrant space for the life that continued to unfold. The photographs of Mae were still there, not hidden away, but integrated into the everyday. These were not painful reminders of absence, but cherished touchstones, tangible links to the love they shared. They were a quiet affirmation that she was not gone, but that her presence had simply shifted, becoming a part of the very air they breathed.

They found themselves increasingly drawn to nature, to the quiet resilience of the natural world. Long walks in the woods, the rustling of leaves underfoot, the ever-changing hues of the sky – these became their therapy. They saw in the steadfastness of the ancient trees, in the persistent growth of wildflowers pushing through concrete, a reflection of their own journey. The cycles of nature, its constant ebb and flow, its capacity for renewal even after winter's harshness, offered a profound sense of hope. It was a silent, unwavering promise that life, in its myriad forms, would always find a way to endure.

The laughter that returned to their home was different now. It was more measured, perhaps, less unrestrained than the ebullient joy of years past, but it was also deeper, more resonant. It was a laughter born of shared experience, of a profound understanding of life's fragility and its inherent beauty. It was the laughter of two people who had faced the abyss and emerged, not unscathed, but with a profound appreciation for the light that still existed. It was a testament to our resilience, a quiet declaration that even in the face of immense sorrow, the human spirit could find its way back to joy.

There was a quiet acceptance that settled over them, a peace that had been hard-won. It wasn't the absence of sadness, but the understanding that sadness was a part of life, a natural consequence of loving deeply. They no longer fought against it, nor did they allow it to consume them. They had learned to hold it, to acknowledge its presence, and to still find the capacity for joy, for connection, for a life rich with meaning. Their journey had been arduous, marked by profound loss, but it had also been a journey of extraordinary growth. They had discovered a strength within themselves, a resilience they never knew they possessed, and a capacity for love that had, in fact, been amplified by our experiences.

www.ingramcontent.com/pod-product-compliance
Lightning Source LLC
LaVergne TN
LVHW010630100826
845148LV00014B/3181

* 9 7 9 8 2 3 4 0 4 3 1 3 9 *